HANDS ON

Debbi Rawlins

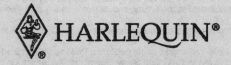

HARLEQUIN®

TORONTO • NEW YORK • LONDON
AMSTERDAM • PARIS • SYDNEY • HAMBURG
STOCKHOLM • ATHENS • TOKYO • MILAN • MADRID
PRAGUE • WARSAW • BUDAPEST • AUCKLAND

This is for Susan Pezzack,
for her keen eye and patience of a saint.
Thank you for being a true writing partner and
helping to keep me on the straight and narrow.

ISBN 0-373-79064-3

HANDS ON

Copyright © 2002 by Debbi Quattrone.

Printed in U.S.A.

Prologue

"I THOUGHT you'd decided not to take that kind of case." Cassie York made herself comfortable across the desk from her new boss, Jennifer Rodriguez Madison.

The phone rang before Jen could respond. She gave Cassie an apologetic smile and grabbed the receiver. "Madison Investigations." She paused. "Today?" She didn't bother checking her full calendar. "How about tomorrow afternoon, say around three?" She rubbed her eyes and yawned away from the phone. "Sorry, that's the soonest I can meet with you, Mr. Rice. I'm squeezing you in as it is."

While Jen got the potential client's details Cassie got up and went to peek at Annie in her portable crib. Her chubby round face looked angelic, but that was because she was sleeping. When she was awake, she had a pair of lungs that could be heard all the way to Dallas.

With operating the new agency, being newly married and raising a child, too, Jen sure had her hands full. Cassie envied her in some ways. Jen not only had it all, but she was making it work, adapting along the way, balancing her time and responsibilities to suit both her career and her family.

Eventually Cassie would get to that place, but first she needed to prove herself. And Jen was about to give her the perfect opportunity.

"Sorry." Jen hung up the phone. "Where were we?"

"You were about to explain Marianne Cummings's case." Cassie returned to her seat.

"Oh, right." Jen pulled out her side drawer, leaned back in her chair and swung her legs up to rest her heels on the drawer. "I have to keep my feet up so they won't swell like two balloons." She rubbed her rounded tummy. "This baby wants out already."

"Don't you have two months to go?"

She nodded, making a funny face.

Cassie laughed. "Sounds as if it's mama who wants that baby out."

"That, too." Jen's lips lifted in a wry smile. "Okay, the Cummings case. This one's important to me, Cass. Marianne is a dear friend, and I personally think the slimeball she married is out for her money and then it'll be *hasta la vista*."

"Ah, so *that's* why you're taking this kind of case."

Jen shrugged. "I have no problem with the decoy tactic. If a guy is happily married and not looking, he won't take the bait. I only turned down the last one because I didn't have enough staff."

At least Jen didn't say she now had a dumb blonde to fit the bill as decoy, Cassie thought. Of course she wouldn't. They'd known each other for three years, and Cassie knew Jen respected her abilities beyond working as a secretary for a rival agency. She was just being touchy. Her experience with Chet had left her that way.

Jen smiled. "I know this is a disappointing case being your first one with us. You were probably looking forward to something meatier, but I really appreciate you jumping in. Like I said, I think Marianne is being taken for a ride. I'm glad she's finally starting to get suspicious of Robert."

"Why? What's he done?"

"Long periods away from home. Says he's on a business trip, but doesn't show any income, secretive about phone calls, and she thinks he has a private mailbox. He's never asked her for money, though, which is a bit of a puzzle."

"She has a lot of it I take it?"

"More than she'll ever be able to spend. Her first husband passed away two years ago and she was left with three homes, a healthy investment portfolio and too much free time to feel sorry for herself. And then up popped Robert Bask, twenty years her junior and as smooth as chocolate silk pie."

Cassie shook her head. The age thing alone wasn't a big deal in her mind, but the rest added up to trouble. "I'll see what I can do. I assume you have some information on his routines and personal habits."

"Right here." Jen picked up a file folder and laid it in front of Cassie. "Of course he hasn't been totally forthcoming about his whereabouts, but she does know he favors this one bar outside of town."

"I'll read this over and start tomorrow." Cassie stood. "Thanks for giving me this chance to join the team, Jen."

"Are you kidding? It's me who should be on my knees thanking you. But I'm sure you'll excuse me if I don't get up," she said with a wry grin and a hand on her tummy.

Annie chose that moment to wake up and let out a huge wail. Jennifer briefly closed her eyes and groaned. "On second thought," she muttered, struggling to her feet.

"I'll get her," Cassie offered.

"Thanks but it's feeding time and that makes me the most popular person in this little lady's life." She made a shooing motion with her hand. "Anyway, I want you to go get started on the case."

"You've got it, boss."

"Call me tomorrow." She picked up her daughter and the baby immediately quieted. "Let me know how you're going to handle the documentation. A wire would probably be best, but I'll let you decide how you want to work it. Although frankly, I think your word will be enough for Marianne to give him the boot."

"Let me think about it, but I'll probably use a wire. I know they haven't been married long, but just in case they end up in court."

"Good thinking." Jen got ready to feed Annie, and Cassie headed for the door. "I'm so glad you've joined us."

Cassie stopped with her hand on the doorknob, pride

filling her chest. She'd do the best damn job possible on this case. Jen would never be sorry she took her in as a rookie. And everyone—Chet, her father, her brother—they'd all see that she was more than just a pretty face.

1

Not only did the new assignment suck, but it had landed J. Dalton Styles in this little Podunk town outside of Midland, Texas. Penance. That was what this was about. For having the balls to get the job done no matter what. And politics. His boss wanted a promotion so bad he could taste it. Just wait till Hector needed a favor. Screw him. He'd have to ask another investigator to do his dirty work.

Dalton took a sip of warm beer. He'd ordered it for show, that's what all the cowboys in the bar seemed to be drinking. But he was on the job, which meant no alcohol. One of the few rules he did adhere to. He'd seen enough good federal investigators lose their careers over drugs or booze.

And women. Bad marriages. Not him. He'd gotten out first.

Shit, who was he kidding? Linda left him for another guy. She'd claimed Dalton worked too much. Hell, he didn't care. Good riddance. A wife and kids would be a burden. He'd been crazy to think he could swing it. That wasn't his scene.

Neither was this assignment.

He drummed his fingers on the bar and looked at

his watch. He'd already been here an hour, sporting this ridiculous Stetson, trying to blend in with the decor. Wearing the cowboy boots was no hardship. He wore one of the three pairs he owned all the time. The guys back in Chicago razzed him. He didn't give a rip. He'd gotten used to them early in his career during his first Texas assignment.

That had been a hell of a good case. His first major bust. Two guys holding a woman hostage at a meth lab near the Mexican border. Dalton had taken them down before the hostage negotiator even arrived.

Eight years and three commendations later, he gets stuck with this fluff assignment. How ironic that he had to expose a con artist who bilked wealthy women out of their divorce settlements. Dalton figured if the women were that stupid to fall for a smooth-talking snake like Robert Bask, they deserved to be left penniless.

Let those rich ladies work for a living. Let them know what it's like to push themselves for long hours, hoping to build a nest egg, telling themselves it was worth it, that someday they could start a family without worrying about making ends meet.

Linda hadn't understood. She was a taker, not a giver. In fact, she'd taken everything but the coffee-maker when she left. And only because the thing didn't work worth a damn.

The front door opened and he casually slid a look at the new arrival. Early thirties, and well-heeled judging by the guy's seven-hundred-dollar snakeskin boots and the gleaming gold Rolex on his wrist. Same yuppie type, but this guy wasn't his boy. Bask had blond hair and stood half a foot shorter.

Dalton rubbed the back of his neck. His source had assured him that Bask stopped here for a shot of tequila most evenings. It would be just Dalton's luck that tonight the guy decided to hop on the wagon.

"How long you gonna nurse that thing?" The bearded bartender threw a towel over his shoulder, put both hands on the bar and leaned forward, staring at Dalton.

"Give me something else." Dalton pretended to study the bottles of booze lined up against the mirror. "How about a shot of that tequila?"

"You got it." The bartender got out a glass and poured a hefty portion of the amber liquid. He set it in front of Dalton. "I've never seen you in here before."

"Nope." Dalton pretended to take a sip, and stopped the guy when he started to remove the beer.

"You waiting for someone?"

"You writing a book?"

The man put both his hands up and stepped back. "Just trying to make conversation, mister."

"Hey, no problem. I'm just a little edgy." Dalton didn't need to piss the guy off. Bartenders were often a good source of information.

The bartender chuckled. "Must be woman problems."

Dalton shrugged. "Something like that."

"I can always spot a rebound a mile away." He nodded smugly as if he'd just solved the crime of the century. "I'm Jerry, by the way. I got a good ear for listening."

Man, he wished the guy would shut up. But then again, maybe he had a big mouth to go with that good ear. "Get me another shot."

Jerry eyed the glass Dalton hadn't touched yet, but shrugged and went to get the bottle of tequila. As soon as he'd turned his back, Dalton emptied the liquor into his beer.

"Whoa! That was fast." Jerry set the clean glass aside and refilled Dalton's empty. "You must be having big trouble with the wife."

He smiled and scoped out the pool table in the corner. Two guys played eight ball while getting shit-faced, even though the tall red-haired, lanky one looked too young to drink. "This is kind of a strange place."

"The bar or the town?"

"Both."

"Yup." Jerry set the bottle of tequila aside and rested both elbows on the bar, leaning closer as if he had a big secret to tell. "This town is made up of the super rich and the poor slobs who made them that way. And nothing in between."

"Odd for such a small town."

"Not really. Lots of big cattle ranches and oil around here. Folks who owned the right piece of property got to be millionaires practically overnight. Most of them are still good ole boys. They've bought themselves fancy cars and boots, but they still come in here to drink beer on tap." Jerry's gaze darted to the newest customer who flirted with the busty waitress, and his voice lowered. "A few got their noses so high in the air it's a wonder they don't get nosebleeds."

Lots of money. Rich widows. Rich divorcées. Perfect breeding ground for Bask. Now it made sense why he'd landed out here. Dalton brought the tequila to his lips and took a small sip for Jerry's benefit. "Guess you don't get many strangers around here."

The bartender shrugged. "Some high-fallutin Dallas types looking to buy oil or beef."

Or con artists. Damn, he wished he could come up with a way to swing the conversation toward Bask without raising a red flag. Jerry could probably give him an earful.

Jerry frowned suddenly. "What kind of business did you say you're in?"

Dalton started to dish out his spiel when the door opened, drawing the bartender's attention. Something inside Dalton jumped. It was Bask. Call it instinct, whatever, but he knew it.

"Wow! Never seen her before." Jerry straightened. "What a looker."

Dalton twisted around. A blonde in tight black jeans and a low-cut black T-shirt stood inside the door and looked around the bar. "Shit," he muttered, and turned around to stare into his beer. He'd been so sure it was Bask.

Jerry narrowed his gaze at Dalton, and then let it wander back to the woman. "You know her?"

"What?" Distracted, Dalton took a sip of the tequila. This sucked. How much longer would he have to sit here?

"Excuse me." The soft feminine voice was somewhere to his left at the other end of the bar. He caught sight of her out of his peripheral vision and started to turn toward her, when she said to Jerry, "I'm looking for a Robert Bask."

Dalton froze, and then he pulled his hat down lower over his eyes and angled the opposite way. Who the hell was this woman? Bask's next target? An accomplice?

"Well, ma'am, I know a Robert but I don't know his last name. I believe he should be showing up at any moment." Jerry was all southern charm. "Can I get you something refreshing to drink while you wait?"

"No, thank you. Oh, wait…maybe a diet cola."

"Yes, ma'am."

"With a squeeze of lime. And a cherry, if you have one."

Dalton slid off his chair as the woman amended her order twice. He headed toward the bathroom, looking for a back door or window. He needed to find out who she was before Bask arrived. Whether she was a mark or about to join the party, Dalton didn't need her screwing up his investigation. Better he knew her role in Bask's scheme.

Opposite the men's bathroom was a door that led out to a short alley. Dalton let himself out quietly and then headed in the direction of the parking lot. Half a dozen cars he recognized. They'd already been there when he arrived. The black Lexus and the red Toyota had to belong to the yuppie and the blonde.

He glanced around, and then laid a hand on the hood of the Lexus. Only moderately warm. Luckily, the Toyota was at the far end of the lot, away from the bar and the street. As he'd suspected, the engine had just been turned off. Had to belong to the blonde. He checked over his shoulder, saw that it was clear, and broke into her car in less than two minutes.

Heavily tinted windows and no security system. Man, was this his lucky day. He slid into the driver's seat, and cursed when he hit his bum knee. The seat was adjusted too far forward for his long legs. She looked to be about five foot five, while he was just over six feet.

He left it the way it was, and checked the visor and then the glove compartment for her registration. He found it stacked neatly with her owner's manual and several maps.

"Cassie York, Midland, Texas," he murmured. Until he ran a check on her, that information did him little good. He rifled through the glove compartment again, and finding nothing helpful, he flipped open the center console.

The small cubicle looked like a survival kit. Candy bars, granola bars, a hairbrush, two tubes of lipstick, a toothbrush in a plastic baggie and a small leather business card holder. He picked it up and read the top card.

"Goddamn!"

A private investigator? He looked out of the tinted

window toward the bar as if he could see the blonde. Cassie York, private investigator.

"Shit!"

She was going to screw everything up. Bask would know his latest con was a bust, and disappear. And Dalton would be stuck following this guy for the rest of his sorry career.

No way. He got out of the car and practically sprinted to the back door. A dark blue Mercedes pulled into the lot just as he let himself in. With his luck, it was probably Bask, just because now he didn't want him to show up.

Dalton swore when he creamed his finger in the door in his haste to get to Cassie York. He had to stop her. Whatever she had planned. No matter what.

CASSIE REALLY HATED playing the dumb blonde. But it worked. Every time. Men could be so stupid. She smiled at the bartender, and then sipped her diet cola from the straw he'd given her. Although it was more a salad bar than a soda. He'd dumped in cherries and orange slices and even a couple of green olives.

She wasn't complaining, though. She'd skipped lunch to get here on time. One flattened Milky Way was all she'd had since her breakfast of dry cereal.

Hell, she'd starve for a week to get this assignment. Her first big case. Okay, so it was her first case, period. But she'd worked as an assistant to Chet, sleazeball private detective extraordinaire, long enough to know what she was doing.

Even Jennifer Madison had faith in her. Hired her

in a heartbeat. Explained what an important case this was, how it was more than just another case, how it was personal. And Cassie wouldn't let her down. As an added bonus, once Cassie cracked the case and put Robert Bask behind bars, she'd rub Chet's nose in it.

She cringed, thinking about the one time she'd slept with him. Had she been out of her mind? Sure, he was good-looking, but he was so full of himself. Of course she'd been only twenty-two, fresh out of college and overly impressed with the well-dressed, fast-living Romeo. At twenty-four she was a lot wiser now.

And cynical.

"Can I get you something else, darlin'?" The bartender gave her a toothy grin.

Darlin'? God, she hated endearments. Especially from strange men. She gritted her teeth and resisted the urge to correct his grammar. Instead, she smiled and leaned forward.

She really hadn't meant to give him a view down her scooped-neck Victoria's Secret T-shirt. "Do me a favor, sugar."

"Sure." The guy eagerly leaned toward her.

She touched the end of his dark beard with the tip of her polished pink finger. "Don't tell Robert I was asking about him."

"Not a word."

No one else had heard her inquire about Bask. Except maybe the man wearing the Stetson who'd been sitting at the bar when she came in. He'd apparently gone to the bathroom and didn't seem to care why she was here. Good thing.

Too late it had occurred to her that she shouldn't have asked about the guy at all. She should have just waited, acted coy once he arrived, waited for him to make a move. Cassie was his type, according to his wife. He liked twenty-something blondes with long hair, not too tall or thin.

But he'd married Jennifer's friend, Marianne, who'd turned fifty-five two months ago, and had never had a blond day in her life. She had money, though, and Robert seemed to like that, too.

Cassie's job was to test his faithfulness. Not her first choice of assignment. But the case was important to her boss. And if the guy turned out to be a gold-digging lothario, Cassie would expose him. With pleasure.

She took another sip of the cola and then fished out a cherry. At the other end of the bar, the waitress placed an order with the bartender, which gave Cassie a small break. The guy had hung around like a dog hoping for scraps.

She scooped out another cherry, polished it off, and then licked the sticky sweetness off her lips. She used the cocktail napkin to blot up the rest.

Pink lipstick smeared the white paper.

Darn it. She'd have to reapply it. Plus, she hadn't checked her hair. It undoubtedly needed to be brushed. She sighed, and slid off the barstool. Some decoy she made.

She hoped the restroom was in the direction the man with the Stetson had disappeared, although he'd been gone a long time. As if her thoughts had conjured him up, he reappeared just as she stepped away from the bar.

Someone opened the front door behind her and sunlight streamed into the dimly lit room, illuminating the man's face. Dark hair, dark eyes, rugged good looks, enhanced by the cleft in his chin.

He looked past her toward the front door, and then stared directly at her.

She averted her gaze and stepped to the side to give him room. Just as she was about to pass him, he grabbed her roughly by the elbows and pulled her against him. His rock solid chest muffled her gasp.

"Baby, I was afraid you wouldn't show up," he said rather loudly.

She pushed away from him, although he held on to her arms. "What the hell do you think you're doing?"

"I'm sorry for walking out last night. I don't blame you for being angry."

That he'd obviously mistaken her for someone else provided some comfort. At least he wasn't some whacko who'd just flipped out. But when he started to walk backward, trying to take her with him, panic seized her.

She kicked him in the shins.

"Shit!" His grip slackened, but before she could jerk away, he regained his hold. He yanked her up close so that she had to tilt her head back to keep her nose from touching his chin. His eyes were dark with warning and sent a shiver down her spine. "Look, honey, I'm trying to say I'm sorry."

What was wrong with these guys in here? Why

wasn't anyone trying to help her? She parted her lips, ready to scream but the man slanted his head and covered her open mouth with his.

She couldn't breathe. She tried to pull away, tried to close her mouth, but he used his tongue to keep her lips parted, her breath trapped in her chest.

His breath was warm and sweet and the kiss surprisingly tender, and for an instant she forgot she was being assaulted. When she finally gathered enough wits about her to try to bite him, he was too quick and eluded her.

His withdrawal gave her the opportunity to call for the bartender. She sucked in a much-needed breath but before she could yell, he whispered, "Wait. I can explain."

Their eyes met. He had incredibly persuasive warm brown eyes. "Let go of me," Cassie demanded.

He hesitated, his dark brows slightly furrowed. "Sorry, I can't do that," he said, and then startled her by picking her up and cradling her to his chest. "I'll be back to settle up, Jerry. The wife and me need to talk outside."

"The hell—"

He silenced her with his mouth, using his tongue to ensure her cooperation as he carried her toward the front door. The bartender winked and waved a hand. They passed the guy who'd walked in a moment ago. He watched them with mild interest, and no inclination to get involved. He looked just like the picture she had of Robert Bask.

The realization subdued her for the moment as her

thoughts scrambled. This Neanderthal in a Stetson had just blown her cover. Bask thought she was married. But maybe that didn't matter to someone like him...

They got outside and panic started to rise again. She twisted her body, and he lost his hold. She started to go down fanny first, but he caught her and set her on her feet.

She stumbled backward. "Stay away from me."

He put his hands up, palms out. "It's not what you think. I'm a federal investigator."

"A what?" She stared in disbelief.

"With the Attorney General's office." He reached into his jacket pocket.

She took another step back. "Don't move or I'll scream loud enough to have half the county come running."

His left brow rose in amusement. "I hope you weren't counting on the half in there."

"I scream and you wanna bet those boys come running?"

He sobered. "I'm reaching into my pocket to get my badge, okay?"

She let out a shaky breath. "You have two seconds."

He promptly withdrew a small leather case, and then flipped it open. One side had a gold badge, the other a picture ID.

"What's your interest in Robert Bask?"

Cassie stared at the badge. It looked authentic enough, and the picture matched. His name was J. Dalton Styles. She looked up into his dark probing eyes.

"I don't care who you are, or who you work for. You had no right manhandling me that way."

His lips lifted in a smirk. "Manhandling?"

"That's right," she said, and slapped him across the face so hard her palm stung. "Now, we're even."

2

"WHAT THE HELL did you do that for?" Dalton rubbed his stinging cheek. The woman was a lunatic.

"You have to ask?"

"Obviously."

"The only thing obvious to me is that our government had better add manners and etiquette to their training programs."

He made a face. She had a great body, pretty face and slight southern accent that would ordinarily inspire thoughts of satin sheets and a good bottle of wine. But the woman was clearly a nut. "What does the government have to do with anything?"

"You work for them, don't you?"

"Ah, Christ, don't— Hey—" He grabbed her arm when she tried to leave. "This is serious. I need to know what your interest in Bask is."

"I'm a private detective."

"I know, but why are you after Bask?"

"What do you mean you know?"

Dalton darted a look toward the bar. No one had come outside but there were two windows from where they could be watched. "I checked you out. Your name is Cassie York and you work for Madison Investigations.''

Her blue eyes widened. ''You couldn't have known that.''

He shrugged. ''Okay, so I don't know about that. Tell me about Bask.''

''I meant, that quick. You couldn't have checked me out. You—'' She glared, her face turning pink. ''Have you been following me?''

''Never laid eyes on you before today.'' Damn, he didn't want to admit he'd broken into her car. No telling what she'd do. ''Look, we don't have much time.''

She folded her arms across her nicely rounded chest producing a fair amount of tempting cleavage. ''Tough.''

He bit back a curse. ''Do you believe I'm a federal marshal?''

She blinked, and uncertainty flickered in her eyes. ''Well, I did, but maybe I shouldn't.''

Christ Almighty. ''You saw my badge. The point is you've got to trust me.''

''Why?''

''Because Bask is scum, and you obviously want him just like I do.''

''Why do you say he's scum? What's he done to get your attention?''

''Can we discuss this later?'' He glanced toward the bar door. ''Before you blow this case?''

Anger flashed in her eyes. ''Me? I'm not the one who picked you up and kissed you.'' Her face got pink again, and she swiped nervously at her hair.

"Shit!"

"There's no need to swear."

"Someone's coming out of the bar." He breathed a sigh of relief. It was one of the guys who'd been playing pool. "It's not Bask. But you know damn well we're being watched."

She glanced over her shoulder. Dalton took the opportunity to check out her goods. But he wasn't fast enough to get away with it.

She gave him a dirty look and pulled up her neckline. "I'm undercover."

"Ah."

Indignation made her eyes round and incredibly blue. "I'm supposed to be bait."

He nodded, annoyed with himself. "Sure, you're working for the wife. I should've figured that out."

"I didn't say that. I can't tell you who I'm working for."

"Look, Cassie, wouldn't it make sense to work together?" he said desperately. He was so close. Days away from finally collaring this guy. And now he had to bargain with this nutty blonde.

She moistened her peach-tinted lips and furrowed her brows. "Work together how?"

Nutty, but damn pretty. Maybe it wasn't a bad idea to use her. Bask would jump at the bait. "I don't know. I gotta figure it out."

She rubbed her arms with misgiving and nibbled at her lower lip. If he didn't know better, he would've thought she was trying to make him crazy. Her lips were perfectly shaped, perfect fullness, and even when she wasn't returning a kiss...

He promptly derailed his thoughts. He didn't need his jeans getting all tight and uncomfortable. Besides, he had some fast thinking to do and that meant blood needed to flow up and not down.

"Look," he said in a low coaxing voice. "At this point, our chances are much better if we work together, however necessary."

The indecision vanished from her face. "By 'at this point' you must be referring to the mess you made in there."

He gritted his teeth, and then forced a smile. "Right."

With a smug curve to her lips, she said, "Okay, I'll work with you as long as it's not anything—weird."

"Define weird."

Concern darkened her face.

"Only kidding." He checked the door again. All clear. "Well, we can't shake on it. We're supposed to be married. Couples who've just made up usually..." he shrugged and tried to keep a straight face "...kiss."

She gave him an unexpectedly sweet smile. "Or maybe we haven't made up. Maybe I'm still angry with you. I could slap your face again."

He reflexively touched his cheek. It still stung. "I'll pass."

Regret briefly clouded her eyes. "What do we do now? Go back in? Wait for him to leave?"

The decision was taken out of their hands. Bask

stepped outside, stopped to put on his sunglasses, and then looked their way.

"Show time."

"What?" Cassie started to turn around.

He grabbed her hands and forced her to face him. "Bask is headed this way. Talk. We need to talk."

"About what?"

"Married stuff."

"Oh, so we should keep arguing then."

He snorted. Obviously she'd been married before. "Follow my lead, okay?"

She hesitated, and then gave a curt nod.

Bask had gotten within a few yards. Dalton pulled her closer and slid his hands around her waist. "Baby, you want to make this marriage work, don't you?"

"Frankly, I'm not sure anymore." She tried to wriggle out of his grasp.

He hauled her against him. "Come on, baby, we're good together. Think about what you'd miss."

She let out a dismissive laugh. "Not much, lately."

He reminded himself this was only playacting. Nothing personal. "Then let me refresh your memory." He slanted his mouth over hers and used her startled gasp to his advantage.

His tongue easily slid between her lips. At first she tensed, and then she opened more to him, her tongue tentatively touching his. She tasted like cherries and oranges and soft feminine mystique. Her soft full breasts pushed against his chest and one of her hands flattened over his chest.

She let out a soft whimper, and Dalton dove deeper,

sliding his hands over her bottom and pulling her harder against his straining fly.

Someone cleared his throat.

Bask.

Shit! Dalton had forgotten about him.

He retreated slowly and met Cassie's glazed eyes. "Did that help your memory, honey?"

She blinked, the fingers of the hand on his chest curling, her nails digging into him. Fire chased the daze look in her eyes. "*This* is what I'm supposed to miss?" Her breathlessness seemed to anger her more.

Made him smile.

"Bastard," she whispered.

Bask cleared his throat again. "Excuse me, folks."

They both looked at him. Cassie did a good job of pretending she didn't know he was there. Her eyes widened and her cheeks got pink.

"I'm sorry to interrupt," Bask said, the megawatt smile that had netted him illegal millions in place. "But I couldn't help overhearing you two in the bar."

"Yeah, so?" Dalton gave the guy a challenging glare.

Bask's smile didn't waver. "I may be able to help."

"Mind your own business, pal." Dalton turned away from him to look at Cassie.

She jerked away from him. "You don't have to be rude to the man. After all, you did cause a scene he couldn't help but overhear."

"*I* caused a scene?"

"Too bad you didn't inherit your mama's manners as well as her money."

Dalton forced back a surprised smile. She was good. "You leave my mama out of this. You never complain about the cushy lifestyle she's provided for you."

"You're right. My only complaint is you." She lifted her chin, turned back to Bask, and gave him a sugary sweet smile. "I must apologize for my husband's rudeness. Please. You were saying?"

Bask homed in on her receptiveness. His body language even changed subtly. He angled toward Cassie and maintained eye contact, even mirroring a couple of her movements, a trick to further put her at ease. The guy was slick. No doubt about it.

"I'd like to give you my business card." He plucked one out of the leather billfold he withdrew from his blue Armani sports coat. "My name is Robert Blankenship and I own Back to Basics."

Before he could actually hand the card off to her, Dalton snatched it out of his hand. "I'll take that."

Cassie made a sound of disapproval.

"Actually, I was planning on giving you each one." Bask presented her with a card and a wide smile, showing off his expensive caps.

"Thank you." She gave Dalton a withering look, and then her gaze lowered to the card.

He'd already read it. Back to Basics was a marriage encounter resort. Bask promoted himself as the facilitator.

What a gig. Dalton had to admit the guy had smarts. How many rich, unhappy divorcées ended up crying on his shoulder while he emptied their pockets?

Cassie looked up at Bask, her blue eyes narrowed

in confusion. Her lips formed this cute little pout that could distract a man from his objective if he weren't careful.

"I don't understand how this could help us." She looked from Bask to Dalton. "What do you do at one of these things?"

Dalton couldn't tell if she really didn't know or if she was acting. He didn't say anything but instead watched Bask spin his web.

"Well, there are usually five couples who go on a kind of retreat for a week. There would be one facilitator there, which would be me, and my assistant who would help guide you through the exercises."

"We're not going on any damn retreat, or doing any exercises. Come on, Cass." Dalton grabbed her arm and tried to steer her away.

She reacted perfectly by jerking away from him. "Did you not just minutes ago say you wanted to save our marriage?"

"Well, yeah, but—"

"Then I suggest you shut up and listen to the man." She turned back to Bask. "Again, I'm sorry. Please go on."

Dalton scrubbed the side of his jaw to hide his amusement. She was really getting into this role, especially when she got to blast him.

"No problem." Bask gave them a combined smile, patronizing and annoying as hell. "I encounter this type of situation all the time. Either the husband or wife, but frankly mostly the husband, is resistant to any kind of therapy."

Dalton groaned. "Therapy."

Cassie gave him a dirty look.

Bask held up a hand. "Let me finish. Once I explain how our method for exploring and stimulating the relationship works, the husband usually comes around."

Dalton glanced at his watch. "You have two minutes."

"We believe that we must address all aspects of the union—spiritual, intellectual and physical. There is a beautiful meditation garden on the premises, a spa and pool and of course the physical contact can be done in private or anywhere for the less inhibited. All group sessions are—"

"Hold it." Dalton's interest peaked. "What do you mean by physical contact?"

Cassie's interest was obviously aroused, as well. She watched Bask with wide anxious eyes.

He shrugged. "Physical contact can mean anything from massaging each other to sexual relations."

Cassie coughed. "In public?"

"That's entirely up to you." Bask produced a reassuring smile. "Of course most couples prefer the privacy of their rooms."

"Now, you're talking." Dalton made a show of studying the card. "You just might be hearing from us, Mr. Blankenship."

Cassie opened her mouth to say something but her expression warned Dalton to cut the conversation short. He threw an arm around her shoulders and kissed her open mouth.

She sputtered.

Dalton gave Bask a leave-the-little-woman-to-me wink. Bask nodded and headed toward the dark blue Mercedes.

"Dammit!" Cassie shoved at Dalton's shoulder when he wouldn't release her.

"Now just calm down. Wait until he leaves before you start kicking up a fuss."

"What I'm going to kick is your behind."

"Fine. After he leaves." Dalton furtively watched him climb into the car. The windows were so heavily tinted he couldn't see the guy. But Dalton figured he was watching them, assessing what sort of candidates they'd make for whatever scheme he'd concocted.

"The hell with that. I'm leaving."

Dalton grabbed her when she tried to go.

"Ouch!"

"I didn't hurt you."

Cassie's lips did that little pouty thing, and she rubbed the area around the wrist that he held. "Yes, you did. You're still hurting me."

He didn't believe it, but he promptly released her. Her smile had "sucker" written all over it. "Trying to make me kiss you again?"

The grin was instantly replaced with a glare. "Dream on."

"It seems that's the only way I get any cooperation out of you," Dalton said, distracted by Bask pulling out of the parking stall and onto the street. "There he goes. Smug bastard."

"We finally agree on something." Cassie stared after the car as it made a turn and disappeared.

"At least I know where I can find him." Dalton studied the card. "Marriage counseling. Pretty friggin' smart."

"Okay." She shrugged. "I guess now you make a call and then go arrest him, huh?"

He looked up in disbelief and stared at her. Obviously she didn't get it. "Not exactly."

She stuck her hands in the pocket of her black jeans. They were so tight he didn't know how she had room for her hands, much less the rock she had on her left ring finger. "What did he do, anyway? I mean, I can pretty much guess but— Why are you looking at me like that?"

"That ring you have on your finger, are you married?"

She shoved her hands deeper into her pockets. "I borrowed it from our client."

"Think she'll lend it to you for another week?"

"Why?"

He looked at the card again. "Do you know how friggin' perfect this is?"

"Why?" she repeated, concern raising her voice.

"Why what?"

"Knock it off, Styles. I want a straight answer."

"Oh, honey." He slid an arm around her and smiled. "If we're going to be married, you're gonna have to call me Dalton."

3

CASSIE SLAPPED at the nightstand, trying to find the alarm. The buzzer screamed relentlessly, until she finally opened one eye and shut the darn thing off.

She checked the time, blinking twice to clear the foggy blur...two-thirty.

Sunlight streamed through her apartment blinds. Okay, so it was afternoon. She knew that.

Yawning and stretching, she tried to focus on the ceiling. Afternoon naps were a rarity for her, but after two sleepless nights she hadn't had much choice. Especially with her big adventure coming up in...

She glanced at the clock again—two-thirty-two. She groaned and rolled over to the edge of the bed. Dalton was picking her up in an hour and a half, and she hadn't even packed yet. Not that she had to take much—T-shirts, shorts, jeans, maybe one casual dress.

Darn it, but she wished she'd talked to Bask herself and not had to rely on Dalton for information about the week they'd spend at Back to Basics. She'd actually tried calling Bask herself after talking to Dalton, but all she got was a recording.

Dalton Styles. The proverbial tall, dark and handsome, with his sable-brown hair and chocolate-brown eyes. And sexy as all get-out with that strong chin that needed a shave. And holy cow! What a kisser!

She exhaled and shoved off the bed, thinking about how hot and insistent his mouth had been two days ago. More than one dream about him picking her up and carrying her away had messed with her sleep.

Good thing he annoyed the hell out of her or the next week would be impossible.

She got out the duffel bag she'd used during her college days. After four years of college plus another one in graduate school before she'd called it quits, the bag had taken a beating. Certainly not appropriate luggage for Mrs. Dalton Styles III. Maybe she ought to make him spring for a pricey Louis Vuitton garment bag.

The thought made her smile. Let him try to bury that in his expense account.

She didn't smile for long. The luggage really was a problem. And since she'd been so busy working and hadn't taken many trips, she hadn't needed anything more. But of course, now that she was a full-fledged investigator, she'd probably have more out-of-town assignments.

The idea warmed her. The traveling part, she could honestly do without. She was Texas born and bred, and she liked it here just fine. But that she was actually flying solo now, and not just working as Chet's assistant, forced to play the dumb blonde when it suited his case, made her giddy with excitement.

The phone interrupted her musings and she stared

at it with the oddest combination of dread and disappointment. Was it Dalton? Had plans changed?

After it rang two more times, she snatched it up before the answering machine came on. "Hello?"

"Cassie, it's Jennifer."

Cassie cringed. She'd left a message for her boss this morning, hoping she wouldn't get it until after Cassie was gone. "Hey, Jen."

"This message you left me about Marianne's case... I don't think I understand it."

Cassie sighed. "You probably do. I'm going undercover."

Jennifer laughed. "What do you mean 'undercover'?"

That hurt. Of course Jen didn't mean anything. She'd probably laughed because the strange turn of events was so unexpected. Jennifer had confidence in her. She wasn't like Chet or any of the others who overlooked Cassie as another pretty but not-so-bright blonde.

"Yesterday Bask showed up at the bar."

"Great. Did he pass the test, or what?"

"More like, or what. The Feds are after him."

"As in FBI?"

"I ran into a federal investigator who's been following Bask. He was afraid I'd blow his investigation so he..." Cassie touched the corner of her mouth. Dalton's kiss still burned on her lips. Stupid. Absolutely crazy to give it a second thought. The man was impossible.

"Cassie, are you there?"

"Yeah." She cleared her throat. "He ended up sabotaging my sting."

"Okay, let's back up. Why is he after Bask?"

"For fraud, basically, except they haven't been able to prove anything yet."

"It doesn't matter as far as we're concerned. I know Marianne. That he's under suspicion will be enough for her to cut him loose. Her attorney can take it from here. Congratulations! I believe you've just successfully closed your first case."

"Wait, I—" Words failed her. Her thoughts were in a sudden jumble stewed with panic and disappointment. "It's not that simple. I can't tell Marianne what I know and blow Dalton's case."

"Dalton? He's the investigator."

"Frankly, he's a pain in the ass, but I wouldn't feel right messing up his assignment."

There was a long pause, and then Jennifer said, "You wouldn't have to. Marianne and her attorney can be discrete while divorce papers are filed and this guy wraps up his case."

Cassie walked with the remote phone to the kitchen for something to drink. Her mouth was suddenly drier than the Sahara. "Except without me, there won't be a case."

"For goodness sakes, why not?"

"See…this is confidential, okay? No telling Marianne."

"Of course not." Jen sounded annoyed.

In the background, the baby started to cry.

"Oops!" Jen cooed something to her daughter. "Cassie, could you hold on a minute?"

"Sure." Gladly. Saved by little Annie. She needed a minute to organize her thoughts.

She poured herself a glass of water but eyed the bottle of chardonnay she'd had in the fridge for God knew how long. Her nerves were shot and she hadn't even officially started her role as Mrs. Dalton Styles yet.

Why wasn't she dancing a jig at the thought of getting out of this assignment? Thrilled at the thought of being able to tell that pompous ass to find some other patsy to play his wife?

Oh, heck, there were a lot of reasons. How much more anticlimactic could her first case be? However, if she were to help Dalton, wouldn't that be good for the agency? Once Bask was arrested, the local news would surely pick up the story.

Due to her pregnancy, Jennifer had had to turn down business. One of the cases had to do with following and baiting a suspected philanderer. The wife who'd tried to hire the agency had been most unhappy that her case was denied. She'd accused Jen of all sorts of things from being a reverse sexist to an elitist who thought infidelity cases were beneath her.

News of the agency's success would absolve them. And then of course, there was Chet. He'd see that Cassie had done a bang-up job all by herself. When he came crawling to her to work for him again, she'd tell him to kiss off.

"I'm back. Sorry." Jennifer laughed softly.

Cassie smiled wistfully. Jen loved being a mom and that job always came first. All her detectives knew and respected that about their boss. Cassie wondered if her turn would ever come. Would she have a baby in her arms to coo to and kiss and cuddle?

Sometimes she thought that would never happen. Most of the guys she knew were still in party mode, into the bar-hopping scene, trying to stretch out another year of college so their parents would continue to foot their bills. A few were okay, just young and uncertain about the future, but a lot of them were jerks. Like Dalton Styles.

That wasn't fair. She didn't really know him. But he had manhandled her.

"Cassie, are you there?"

"I was just thinking about how good this is going to look for the agency when we help catch someone the Feds apparently have been after for a long time."

Silence, and then Jen sighed. "What do you know about this Dalton guy? I assume you saw his identification?"

"Of course. I also checked him out. He was recruited out of college eight years ago. He's earned numerous citations and two commendations for bravery and going beyond the call of duty."

"Hmm, this seems like an odd case for someone of his caliber to be assigned to."

Jen was too damn smart. Cassie leaned a hip on the kitchen counter and took a sip of water. She'd decided to skip the part about the reprimands Dalton had received for being a maverick, and for bending the rules as casually as you'd bend a straw. Jen didn't need to worry.

"It doesn't make sense," Jen continued. "Bask isn't supposed to be dangerous, is he?"

"No. He's a snake who swindles lonely, vulnerable women out of money, but he has no history of violence."

"Tell me again about this plan you and Dalton devised."

"We're going to pretend we're married and go for marriage counseling at Bask's retreat."

"How will that expose him?" Jen was obviously holding the baby. Gurgling noises came across the line.

"Dalton thinks that Bask sniffs out a weak marriage where the woman would be vulnerable to him, and then manipulates the couple to split them up while getting the wife to become more and more dependent on him."

"Yeah, okay. I can see that." Jen paused to whisper something to the baby who was beginning to fuss. "Your message said something about possibly being gone for a week?"

Cassie briefly explained the encounter week, carefully editing out the parts that would put her and Dalton into intimate contact. The more she tried to leave out, the more she realized she was crazy for agreeing to this ruse. Not just crazy, terrified.

She would be stuck out in the middle of nowhere for a week with a man she couldn't stand. A man whose kiss made her want to wrap her legs around his waist and not come up for air for a month.

Oh, God, this was not good.

"Cassie, I'm going to have to call you later. Annie needs to be changed."

"Sure." She hung up the phone with a shaky hand, her thoughts already elsewhere. It wasn't too late. She could call Dalton and cancel. He was a resourceful guy. He could make his case without her.

She picked up the phone again and called the Marriott where he was staying, growing impatient when it rang too many times.

She wouldn't let him talk her out of changing her mind. If he thought he could, he had another think coming. When Cassie York made up her mind, that was that.

"ARE YOU SURE you wrote these directions down correctly?" She stared at the scribble on the pad of Marriott paper. "Or maybe you just can't read your own handwriting."

"I can read it fine." Dalton made a U-turn, their third of the afternoon. At this rate they'd be lucky to find the place by dark. "Obviously you don't know a map from a grocery list."

"That was a very sexist remark."

"What? Men don't shop?"

Cassie picked up her water bottle and uncapped it. "You can't blame this on me. I wanted to stop at that gas station five miles back to ask for directions. But nooo...you don't need to ask for help. You know exactly where you're going. Ha!"

She tipped the bottle up to her lips, tempting him to

slam on the brakes and watch her get drenched. If she was practicing her role as a wife, she was doing a damn fine job. She hadn't stopped annoying him since they'd left Midland two hours ago.

"Do you want some water?"

He looked over at her. Damn, but she had pretty eyes. "Is that a trick question?"

Her sandy-colored brows dipped in a confused frown.

He was pretty sure she was a natural blonde. He was good at knowing that kind of stuff. "Why are you suddenly being so nice?"

Her confusion turned to surprise. "*Suddenly* being nice? I've been nothing but gracious and patient."

He laughed.

"I'm serious."

"You've criticized my driving. Steered us in the wrong direction twice. Took too friggin' long at the convenience store just to irritate me—"

"Right. Everything I do is about you. You have saturated my thoughts. Taking too long in the store had nothing to do with the cash register jamming. It was all part of my master plan to irritate you."

"And you talk too much. I don't need a dissertation."

"Screw you. Is that succinct enough?"

He smiled. "When?"

"That is so juvenile. I haven't heard that comeback since junior high."

"When was that? Last year?"

"Gee, another original."

He shook his head with disgust. God help the man who ended up marrying her.

"Now, would you like some water, or not?" She reached into the small cooler she'd brought and got out another bottle of water.

"Yeah, I'll have some."

She surprised him by uncapping it before she handed the bottle to him. "You're welcome."

"Jeez, give me a chance. I was gonna say thanks."

"Oh, wait." She waved a hand excitedly, and he jammed on the brakes. "You're missing the turn again."

"What the hell are you doing? Don't yell like that." He took his foot off the brakes. "I thought I was about to hit something."

"I didn't yell."

No way was he going to respond. She was a nut, three French fries short of a Happy Meal. "By the way, I didn't miss the turn the first time. You forgot to tell me to turn, if you recall."

"But you knew where you were going, remember? You didn't need to ask directions."

He glanced over at her just as she folded her arms across her chest. She had on another one of those scooped neck T-shirts like she wore the other day, only this one was a peach color that matched her jeans.

With her arms crossed as they were, the tops of her breasts plumped up above her neckline. She didn't have a really big chest, but she was nicely rounded and perky. Just enough to make him crazy.

He forced his attention back to the road where it

belonged, but then after a couple of seconds took one more look.

Cassie made a prissy sound. "What are you looking at?"

"I was thinking…maybe we ought to pull over and neck for a while."

Her lips parted in disbelief and she shifted closer to her door.

"You know, just to get used to each other so we'll be convincing once we get there."

"Are you insane?"

He smiled. "Come on. Admit it. You want me."

"How often does the government give their employees psychological tests?"

He laughed and then took a sip of water.

"You are one sick puppy." She relieved him of the bottle.

He saw a sign for Bedrock and got serious. "We should be there in about twenty minutes. Let's review our story."

She nodded. "We've been married for only six months after meeting on a Caribbean cruise."

"That was good thinking on the short time span for knowing each other. That'll give us some leeway in case we botch our stories."

Her lips curved in a pleased smile. "And thank *you* for thinking about the luggage. I'll keep it in as good condition as possible."

"No problem. It's yours to keep for your help."

"But it's so expensive. I can't keep it. No way."

Dalton slid her a surprised glance. She meant it. She

was willing to return a no-strings-attached gift. "Let's get back to our story. I'm from Chicago, went off to Princeton and stayed in the East for a while, got married, divorced...we met on the cruise and after we got married I moved back to Texas at your insistence."

She laughed. "At my insistence, huh?"

"You're the one who's from here. Why else would a born and bred Chicago boy move to Texas?"

She gave him a dry look. "You don't have any sort of accent. Maybe we should say you're from Dallas."

"Better to stick as close to the truth as possible. That way we won't get tripped up."

"I suppose..."

"Why would it be important that I'm from Dallas?"

"You did say that I'd probably get the most grilling from the others, and I agree. Women talk about that kind of stuff, and men usually don't. So since I would never marry someone from Chicago I'm just trying to customize the situation to what's comfortable."

He frowned. Surely he'd heard wrong. "You would never marry anyone from Chicago?"

"That's right."

"Dare I ask why?"

She straightened and pointed. "There's our turn."

He saw the Back to Basics sign just in time to steer the rented Jag down the long winding drive. "You have your story straight?"

"Like you said, I'm sticking to the truth, mostly anyway. I lived in Midland until I went to college. I graduated from Texas A&M two years ago with a degree in psychology. I've had a few different jobs, nothing substantial. I was still finding myself when I met you.''

He wondered which was the mostly true part. Was she still trying to find herself? He knew so little about her. Although he'd had one of his buddies back at the bureau pull a profile on her, he'd carefully stuck to general information, only asking about anything that pertained to the case and her ability to contribute.

About a quarter mile down the drive, a stately white mansion sprung up out of nowhere. Made sense that it was a home Bask had rented and called a resort. Easy to get out and hit the road when the time came.

''Are we in the right place?'' Cassie squinted at the three-story house. ''That looks more like a southern plantation home, certainly a private residence.''

The small discrete sign came into view informing them they were just where they were supposed to be. The front lawn stretched beyond the sign, the entire area loaded with flowers in reds and purples and golds. Dalton didn't much care about flowers one way or the other, but it was a pretty awesome sight.

He glanced at Cassie. ''Are you nervous?''

She shook her head, but her wide-eyed gaze and the way she wrung her hands concerned him. ''This is the best-case scenario for a sting. Bask came to us.''

''I know. Anyway, this is going to be a piece of cake. I don't even have to pretend I like you.''

He snorted and rolled his eyes.

She seemed too distracted to notice. ''Can you believe the size of those lavender roses? And the hedges of heather, my goodness.'' She finally looked at him.

"Another thing you should know about me, I love to garden. I'm already itching to stick my fingers in the dirt and swipe some clippings."

Now, this was a surprise. He hadn't figured her for the hands-in-the-dirt type.

"Why are you looking at me like that? I'm not going to *really* swipe clippings."

"I don't even know what a clipping is." He steered the car into the circular drive. The garages were probably around the back but this seemed like the logical thing to do so they could unload their luggage. Besides, having to move the car later would give him the opportunity to nose around.

Shrill laughter came from somewhere on the side of the house. They both twisted around for a look. A tall redhead opened the white trellis gate and ran through the garden in a tiny bikini bottom, no top, her enormous breasts bouncing with her laughter. Behind her a bare-chested man gave chase.

"Oh, boy," Cassie swung around to look straight ahead. "Okay, now I'm nervous."

4

"IS THERE SOMETHING you forgot to tell me?" Cassie glared at Dalton. "I'm not getting out of this car until you explain to me what just happened. And then, frankly, I probably still won't get out."

He watched the couple disappear on the other side of the house. "I have no idea." He looked at Cassie, his expression one of such surprise that she believed him. "I swear to God I don't."

She hunched down in the seat. "This looks more like a swing club."

"Let's not jump to conclusions."

"What's there to jump to? She was naked. Outside for anyone to see."

"She was topless, not naked."

"Oh, excuse me. That makes a difference. I'm not getting out of this car."

"Cassie, come on, you can't quit now."

"This has nothing to do with quitting." She folded her arms across her chest. The woman probably had implants. Nobody was that big for real. *Were they?*

"Guess you just don't have what it takes to be an investigator. My mistake."

Her heart plummeted, and then she realized what he

was doing. "Nice try, Styles. Psychology 101 has nothing on you."

A knock on the car window drew both their attention.

A young blond woman, about Cassie's age, motioned for Dalton to put his window down.

The woman then stood back, waiting for him to comply. She wore short shorts and a tucked-in pink T-shirt that showed off another pair of large breasts. "You must be Mr. and Mrs. Styles?"

Cassie glanced down at her own B-cups while Dalton replied.

They were perfectly nice breasts. Just not very large.

"My name is Mary Jane." Smiling, with a flawless set of white, straight teeth, she opened his door. "I'm Mr. Blankenship's assistant. Welcome to Back to Basics."

"So we are at the right place," Dalton said as he got out, and Cassie stayed put.

Mary Jane glanced over her shoulder toward where the couple had disappeared, and then made a face when she looked back at Dalton. "I'm sorry about that. I'll have a word with Simone. She's European and insists on sunbathing and swimming topless, which is fine, but she shouldn't have left the pool area like that."

Dalton ducked his head to meet Cassie's eyes. He gave her a meaningful look. "Honey, are you getting out?"

Swimming and sun bathing topless was fine? Right.

She started when her door opened. Mary Jane had come around the car and opened it.

"We have a very special room set up for you and Mr. Styles. I'll take you both inside and then I'll get your luggage."

"Call me Cassie."

"Of course, whatever you prefer." Mary Jane had never stopped smiling, reminding her of a Stepford wife. She stepped back to give Cassie room.

Cassie got out of the car and gave Dalton a look that said, This better not be weird.

"If you follow me I'll give you a tour of the house, point out the common areas where we socialize. Some of the rooms are used for private business, of course. But I'm sure that's of no interest to you."

Cassie and Dalton exchanged looks. Wrong. The private quarters were of far more interest. Excitement began to simmer inside Cassie. This was a real case. Big enough that it had attracted the attention of the government. And she'd landed right smack-dab in the middle of the action.

Dalton was right. Why jump to conclusions about this place? Why let a topless woman derail her?

Mary Jane came up alongside Cassie and hooked an arm through hers, and then hooked her other arm around Dalton's. She flashed a grin at both of them. "Are we ready?"

"Lead on," Dalton said, and winked at Cassie.

It was a very intimate wink, a kind of shared joke, giving Cassie a funny feeling.

"You're gonna love it here. I promise. We have hot

tubs and saunas and an Olympic-size pool.'' Mary Jane chattered all the way up the stairs and into the beautiful hardwood foyer. ''All your meals will be healthy and nutritious and prepared on the premises.''

Dalton grunted and disengaged himself from Mary Jane. ''We better not be talking sprouts and wheat germ.''

Mary Jane laughed and lightly jabbed him with her elbow. ''You're so funny.'' And then she pranced on ahead of them.

Dalton frowned at Cassie. ''Was that a yes or a no?''

She shrugged.

''I eat meat. I like meat.''

''Healthy doesn't mean fanatic.'' She smiled and followed Mary Jane, but tossed over her shoulder, ''Don't jump to conclusions.''

He muttered something she couldn't hear. Didn't want to hear. Instead, she listened to Mary Jane point out the parlor where everyone gathered before dinner.

''Cocktails are usually served around six.'' She glanced at her Mickey Mouse watch. ''Which is in about fifteen minutes. Perfect. You can meet everyone then.''

''You mean real cocktails?'' Dalton asked with narrowed-eyed suspicion. ''Not like carrot juice or anything like that?''

Mary Jane giggled and glanced at Cassie. ''He's so funny.''

Cassie couldn't help laughing herself. She didn't dare look at the expression on Dalton's face, or she'd really lose it. Her nerves were taut, her emotions running high and she knew herself. She was likely to break out into hysterics.

"Over here is the dining room where you'll have your meals, or sometimes we eat on the patio. We'll even send you room service if there's, you know, something special going on you'd rather not interrupt."

"Great." Cassie forced a smile, and refused to look at Dalton. "Can we see our room now?"

He came up alongside her and captured her hand. "Anxious, honey?"

She rolled her eyes, and realized Mary Jane saw her. "Dalton has been sleeping on the couch for the past week. I'd like to maintain that arrangement."

Mary Jane shook her finger. "Now, now. That's why we're all here. To smooth out our differences."

Cassie pursed her lips in thought, and then said, "Tell me, Mary Jane. Have you ever been married?"

The woman laughed. "You're funny, too. Now, we're going upstairs. Follow me."

Dalton put his lips close to Cassie's ear. "I guess we're both just hilarious."

His warm breath tickled the sensitive skin on the side of her neck and she shivered. He gripped her hand tighter. She hadn't realized he still held it.

She pulled away, just as Mary Jane stopped midway up the stairs and turned around. "You'll have to hurry if you want to make the cocktail hour and meet the others."

Cassie moved ahead of Dalton. "They'll be wearing clothes, I trust."

Mary Jane smiled. "I promise," she said, and resumed climbing the stairs.

Her shorts were so short they left nothing to the imagination. In fact, Cassie caught glimpses of a naked cheek, which meant Mary Jane was wearing no underwear or a thong. Dalton had the same view. She wanted to turn around to see his reaction, but she didn't dare. He'd probably think she was jealous.

After making it up to the midpoint herself, she realized he hadn't followed. She looked over her shoulder to find him still standing at the bottom of the stairs. Staring at *her* butt.

He lifted his gaze to meet hers. "I'm going to get the bags from the car and meet you up there."

Mary Jane stood on the landing and leaned over the rail. "I'll take care of that."

"The bags are heavy. I'll only be minute."

"Well, okay…" Mary Jane made a face. "But leave the keys in the car so I can move it to the garage later."

He shook his head. "Nobody drives that baby but me."

Mary Jane gave him one of her toothy grins. "I'll only be behind the wheel for a minute. The garages are directly in back."

"Then I'll just go ahead and do it myself before I bring in the bags." Dalton dug the keys out of his pocket. "I'll find you."

Clearly displeased, Mary Jane watched Dalton retrace their steps. With the sunny disposition gone, she looked a little hard, older, too. She realized Cassie was staring at her and she immediately flashed a smile.

"He's very stubborn," Cassie said as she met her on the landing. "That's why we have so many problems."

"Well, that's exactly what you're here for. Hopefully, by the end of the week, you'll have a better understanding of each other. Robert, uh, Mr. Blankenship is very good at pinpointing problem areas in the marriage."

"Hell, I can do that. I knew this trip was a waste of time. Maybe I ought to tell Dalton to leave those bags right in the car." Cassie folded her arms across her chest and pretended to look out the window for Dalton. Out of the corner of her eyes, she watched Mary Jane's expression get ugly. Oh, she was in on Bask's scheme, all right.

"Now, you're being hasty. Isn't saving your marriage worth one week of your time?" She was all smiles again when Cassie turned to her.

"I suppose." Cassie sighed in her best put-upon wife imitation. "Let's go see our room."

"Right this way." Mary Jane threw one final look toward the front door and then led Cassie down to the end of the hall. "You have a corner room with a view of the pool and gardens," she said, opening the door. "It's the best one, in my opinion."

She stood aside while Cassie preceded her. The room was large, really large, with lots of windows and French doors that led to a verandah. Two large vases of fresh flowers had been set out on the antique mahogany desk nestled in the corner of the sitting area, and the white vanity table and chair close to the window. The queen-size sleigh bed was antique, as were the cherry nightstands and armoire.

The burgundy and cream décor was plush and gorgeous, like a suite at the Ritz, and Cassie caught herself just in time. Her mouth had nearly dropped open. But she was supposed to be rich. This should be no big deal to her.

She tried to look bored. "Don't we have a small fridge or something to keep bottled water cold?"

"Right here." She went to the corner and pulled back a folding panel that looked to be made of raw silk. "You have an entire wet bar, fully stocked."

"Fine." Cassie ducked her head into the bathroom. Under a skylight was an enormous tub surrounded by a blue marble floor.

Mary Jane came up behind her. "The tub is also a whirlpool bath. And of course there's a glass shower stall over there."

"Very nice." Cassie fingered the emerald green velour towels and asked casually, "Does Mr. Blankenship own this house?"

"He leases it."

"It's a lovely home."

"Yes, elegant but homey. Perfect for our clientele. Oh, and did I tell you there's a large walk-in closet?" Mary Jane opened a narrow door and gestured inside. "It's stocked with plenty of hangers, but let me know if you need more."

Cassie looked inside as she was expected to. "Has Mr. Blankenship been running this place long?"

The other woman's brows pulled together in a slight frown and she seemed to briefly assess Cassie. "I don't know. I've only been with him for a few months. Your husband seems to be taking a long time."

Cassie waved a dismissive hand, privately wondering about Dalton himself. "He's probably wiping down his new toy. His mother just bought him the Jag." She sighed dramatically. "I'm a little nervous about being here."

Mary Jane's expression softened. "Everyone is nervous at first."

"Frankly, even though I was the one who pushed Dalton into this, I don't know anything about Mr. Blankenship. Like how long he's been doing this…his success rate…or anything."

Understanding registered in Mary Jane's eyes. If Cassie's questions had made her suspicious, the crisis was over. "Don't worry. Really." She wrinkled her nose. "I can't quote statistics, but I know that most couples leave here with renewed interest in each other. Of the repeats, four out of five marriages remain intact."

"Repeats?"

"You know, after a month or so, most couples come back for a refresher course."

Oh, brother. Cassie's stomach flipped flopped. One week here was bad enough.

Mary Jane started for the door. "Where is that husband of yours?"

"Here I am." Dalton appeared in the doorway suddenly. "You girls miss me?"

"Girls?" Cassie gave him an arched look.

"What? Is that politically incorrect?" He shrugged, directing a wink at Mary Jane as he set down their two suitcases.

Cassie made a sound of exasperation. "See why I need a couch for him?"

He gave her a private warning look. "Come on now, honey, you aren't going to start that again."

Mary Jane smiled and then looked at her watch. "Oops! Cocktail hour has started. Freshen up, and then come on down and meet the group." She closed the door on her way out.

"The closet is over there." Cassie pointed and then headed for the bathroom.

"Excuse me."

She glanced at him.

"Are you expecting me to carry your bag to the closet? Wouldn't that be politically incorrect?"

She put a hand on her hip. "Did I ask you to carry it?"

He smiled and picked up her bag along with his. "Don't get huffy. It was only a question."

"Do you want the bathroom first?"

"No, you go ahead." Ignoring her curt tone, he added, "See, we can be pretty civil when we put our minds to it."

He signaled something with his eyes she didn't understand. But it would have to wait. Nature called insistently. She slipped into the bathroom and closed the door. After she'd taken care of the important business, she splashed her face with water that wasn't nearly as cold as her feet.

What was she so nervous about? Everything was going smoothly. Mary Jane was a bit of an airhead, which worked to their advantage. From all reports, Bask shunned violence. If anything went wrong, and he got suspicious, he'd be the first one to hit the road.

So why was she so edgy? Even if they were discovered, Dalton was here. He had a lot of experience. He could easily handle any physical confrontation.

Oh, God. Talk about being an airhead. *Dalton* was the problem. No more denying it.

She gave her face another dousing before she dried off. How could she possibly find that aggravating man so sexy? Sure, he had great biceps. With the way his polo shirt hugged his arms, anyone would notice. Just like the fit of his snug jeans. Of course she'd taken note of his great butt. Any red-blooded woman would.

She groaned and threw the towel back on the rack. She'd have to get out both her hairbrush and toothbrush before she went downstairs. For now she combed her fingers through her hair. It hung limp from the humidity but she wasn't trying to impress anyone. She gave it an extra fluff and then opened the door.

Dalton was sprawled out across the bed. Not just on one side, but more in the middle. He grinned and patted the side closest to her. "Great mattress. Come try it out."

She swallowed. "I'll flip you for it."

"Cassie..." He drawled her name like a warning.

"Heads you get the bed. Tails you get the floor."

"Come on, honey." Before she could respond, he put a silencing finger to his lips, and crooked his other one, beckoning her to come closer.

She hesitated at first, but he looked serious, not like he was baiting her, so she carefully sat on the edge of the mattress. He shook his head and motioned for her to move closer. She inched in, and leaned toward him.

He cupped the back of her neck and drew her close to his face. "I think the room is bugged," he whispered.

"Are you kidding?" She spoke too loudly and he put a finger to her lips. She had the ridiculous urge to suck it into her mouth, and she tried to move back.

He held her firmly in place. "Come on, honey, just a quickie like the old days. Those people will still be down there." And then in a voice so low she could barely hear, he said, "Just play along. Anything you have to say they shouldn't hear, you'll have to get real close like this and whisper."

He'd pushed back her hair, his lips brushing the side of her ear as he spoke. Goose bumps surfaced on her skin. She'd absolutely die if he saw them.

"Where did you see the bugs?"

He cupped her cheek with his slightly roughened palm and guided her closer, until her lips grazed his jaw and she put a hand on his chest for balance. "I couldn't hear you," he whispered.

"I said, where did you see the bug?"

"Actually, my decoder ring sensed it."

She blinked. His what? Under her palm, his chest shook with laughter. She bolted upright. "You ass!"

"Cassie, wait." He grabbed her hand when she tried to get up, and yanked her unceremoniously against him. "I really think the room is bugged. That was stupid and immature of me. I apologize."

She glared at him. He looked serious again, and he kept his voice at a whisper, but how could she believe him now? How could she afford not to?

"Immature is an understatement."

"You're right." He gave her leg a patronizing pat, which only made her angrier.

"Frankly, I don't know if I believe you," she said, but kept her voice down.

"I don't blame you." He looked so earnest. "I wish I could take it back." Of course, he *was* playing a role. He could be acting right now. "Can we discuss this later? Outside, maybe, and err on the side of caution for now?"

He stroked the inside of her wrist, a slow seductive motion that made her lose track of her thoughts. She shifted away, trying to gain some balance, and he released her. "All right. Later. Now what about the bed?"

"It's pretty comfortable."

She remembered to keep her voice down just in time. "You know what I mean."

"Why would either of us have to sleep on the floor?"

"I know how we can do this fairly. We'll alternate. You get the bed one night, and I get it the next."

"This is something else we should discuss later." He rolled off the bed before she could tell him there was nothing to discuss.

For that he'd get the first night on the floor. "Where are you going?"

"To the john. Okay? And then we'd better get our butts downstairs to happy hour."

She bit back a pithy remark and slid off the other side of the bed. The bathroom door closed as she entered the closet in search of her cosmetics case. By the time she located it, brushed out her hair and applied some tinted moisturizer to her face, Dalton came out of the bathroom. His hair was slightly damp in front, and a bead of water clung to the cleft in his chin. The horrifying impulse to lick it off had her quickly side-stepping him.

He drew back as if he thought she'd run him down. "Ready I take it?"

"In a minute. I have to brush my teeth." Now, why did she tell him what she was going to do? It was none of his business. This was impossible. How could she share a room with this man for a week? He was a stranger. A sexy stranger. It was just too weird.

"Okay, but hurry up."

She didn't say a word. Tempting as it was. She wanted to get the initial meetings over with, as well. The quicker they could get outside for a walk, establish the ground rules, like how he got the floor tonight, and who got the bathroom when.

Maybe she'd just tell him how it was going to be. Why shouldn't she call the shots? He needed her to close this case. She didn't need him. Like Jen had pointed out, they had all the information they needed to satisfy their client.

She opened the door, ready to tell him like it was.

And she would have done exactly that.

If he weren't naked.

5

"WHAT THE HELL ARE YOU DOING?" Cassie's eyes were so wide Dalton thought she'd hurt herself. Her gaze roamed down his bare chest, to waist level, and then she did an abrupt about-face. "We're supposed to go downstairs."

"I know." He slid a white cotton oxford off the hanger. "I'm just changing my shirt. What's the matter with you?"

"This isn't going to work."

"Hey." He shrugged into the shirt but didn't bother to button it as he quickly stepped around the armoire and crossed the room. "Careful," he whispered, taking her by the arms and trying to turn her around to face him.

She wouldn't budge. "Me? You pull a stunt like this and you tell me to be careful."

"What stunt? Why won't you turn around?"

"Are you decent?"

He frowned, and then looked down at his unbuttoned shirt. "You're kidding, right?"

"How would you like it if I—never mind. Just tell me if you've got your clothes on."

"Yeah, I have clothes on." He shook his head. She was a total nut.

Slowly, she turned around, her cautious gaze dropping below his waist. "What were you doing?"

"I told you I was changing my shirt." He saw the accusation in her eyes and prepared for a preemptive strike.

"But you—"

He slid his arms around her waist and drew her close. "Keep your voice down."

Her hands landed on his bare chest and her fingers stiffened. "You haven't buttoned your shirt yet."

"Do it for me."

"Do it yourself."

"You're the one who wants the damn thing buttoned."

At his abrupt tone, her eyes widened. "I'm the one who should be upset. I come out of the bathroom and you don't have anything on. What am I supposed to think?"

At least she kept her voice down. Her gaze roamed his face, and then lingered on his mouth. He wondered if she had any idea how expressive her face was, or that her hand flexed on his chest.

"I still had my pants on. I was only changing my shirt." He glanced over his shoulder. "The armoire must have blocked your view and you assumed I didn't have anything on. I assure you that I will only be naked in front of you if you want me to be." He dropped his hands from her waist.

She didn't move, didn't even take her hand off his chest. "I—I'm sorry."

"No problem. Now, are you gonna button my shirt?"

A small gasp escaped her. She moistened her lips and moved her hand. With her eyes kept lowered she said, "You have a really nice chest."

That stopped him. He wished he had something clever or witty to say. Nothing came to mind. "Thanks." He cleared his throat and went for his top button. "That's okay. I'll do it."

"No." She stilled his hands and then tugged them away. "I will."

Hell, when had he lost control of the situation? He sucked in his belly when she dragged her finger down his chest to his waist. She lingered at his belt, tucking the tip of one finger under his buckle.

He lifted his gaze to meet hers, and then fixed on the slight part of her lips, the tongue darting out to moisten them in invitation. He tilted his head to the side to accept her offer.

"Ouch!" He jumped back and put a hand on his belly to soothe the sting. "What the hell did you do that for?"

"Don't be a baby. I didn't pull that hard." She stepped back and combed a hand through her hair as if nothing had happened. "Just enough to get your attention."

He rubbed the area over his navel where she'd plucked out a couple of hairs. It didn't really hurt.

He'd been surprised more than anything. "Sweetheart, you already had my attention."

"The wrong kind. Get my point?"

He quickly buttoned his shirt. "You came on to me, chickened out and now you're pulling this act. I get the point, all right."

She made a sound of exasperation and glanced heavenward as she headed for the door. "In your dreams."

"We've been married a little too long for you to start acting coy now."

She stopped, turned and stared at him.

He put a warning finger to his lips. He knew he should feel guilty for making up the lie about the bugs in their room, but he hoped this would keep Cassie on her toes.

Cassie blinked, but then without skipping a beat, said, "That isn't coy, that's regret. For marrying you."

"Now that you've got that off your chest, shall we go down and join the others?"

Her response was to open the door and leave without him.

He easily caught up with her before she hit the stairs. "How did it go with Mary Jane while you were alone with her?"

She slid him a peevish look, but then followed his lead and they were back to business. "It's possible she's cagey and playing us, but I think she's just a gofer and frankly, not all that bright."

"You guys didn't talk about anything meaty then?"

Hesitating, her gaze darted away, making him nervous. "Not really. I tried to ask about Bask but she got a little guarded."

He heard laughter coming from the parlor and he stopped midway down the stairs. "As in suspicious?"

Cassie shook her head. "More defensive, especially after I made it sound like I was concerned about his credentials and success rate."

"Good. By the way, don't refer to him as Bask just in case we're ever overheard. Let's just call him Robert."

"Good point."

He smiled. Well, that was something…her actually conceding he had a worthwhile thought.

"What?"

He shrugged. "I'm glad we agree on something."

She gave him a skeptical look and then started to descend the stairs again. "I'm not particularly worried about Mary Jane but I won't be letting my guard down around her either.

"Good. Never underestimate anyone. Do you think she's a natural blonde?"

"Excuse me?" Cassie stopped on the next step, anger simmering in her gaze.

"Now what did I say?"

"She's blond so she has to be dumb?"

"Oh, no." Dalton shook his head and started down the stairs again. "I did not say that."

She was right beside him. "That's what you implied."

"For your information, I only asked because I'm going to give my office a description of her and if either of us thinks she's altered her appearance in any way, which I personally believe she has, I'll need to tell them."

"Oh." The sheepish look on her face did his heart good. "Sorry."

"Hey, did you hear the one about the guy who gave his blond wife a cell phone for Christmas?"

The indignation was back on her face again, and she glared at him. "I have heard every stupid dumb blonde joke there is and none of them are funny."

"You haven't heard the cell phone one, I bet."

"And the ones I haven't heard I don't wish to hear. Thank you very much."

"This will make you laugh. Loosen you up some."

"I'm loose enough."

He grinned. "Just the way I like my women."

"Gee, I'm so surprised."

"Okay, this guy gave his wife a cell phone for Christmas, explained to her how to use it and—"

"I'm not listening."

"The next day she went shopping so he thought he'd surprise her with her first call." Dalton chuckled when she started humming to drown him out. "The wife answered the phone, and totally amazed, asked 'How did you know I was at Wal-Mart?'"

Cassie pressed her lips together.

He gave her a playful nudge. "Tell me that isn't a good one."

"It sucks."

"That's why you're trying not to smile."

"Grow up." She lifted her chin and moved ahead of him.

The noise level from the parlor rose as they got to the bottom of the stairs. Mary Jane appeared with a wineglass in each hand.

She gave them a blinding smile and handed them each a glass. "It's about time you two got down here. Everyone's anxious to meet you."

Dalton stared at the amber liquid. "What is this?"

"Sherry."

"Oh, man." He got a whiff and passed it back to her a bit too forcefully. "No, thanks."

Both women gave him funny looks. So maybe he overreacted, but his ex drank that stuff and he couldn't even stand the thick sweet smell.

"We have a full bar," Mary Jane said. "Just follow me."

"I'm sure they have some rubbing alcohol for you," Cassie whispered with a sugary smile, and then cut in front of him to follow Mary Jane into the parlor.

He was going to have to have a long talk with Cassie about her animosity toward him. She was carrying this sparring marriage act to the limit. He'd explained why he had to kiss her and pick her up in the bar. There was no reason to cop this attitude.

"Here we are," Mary Jane said as they entered the parlor. Everyone stopped talking as six pairs of curious eyes focused on them. "These are our newest guests, Dalton and Cassie Styles. And now I'll let each of you introduce yourselves."

Dalton's gaze immediately went to the redhead. Except regrettably, now she had on a shirt, though low-cut and leaving her midriff bare.

She gave him a dazzling smile. "I'm Simone." She pursed her lips in a pout. "I am so sorry about this afternoon," she said, her voice slightly accented and totally without remorse. "I promise it will not happen again."

Too bad. He smiled. "No problem."

"I'm Grant, her husband."

Dalton had to swing around to link the voice to the man because it sure wasn't the guy sitting next to her. Close, practically on her lap.

Grant stood near the bar, tall, black hair with a touch of gray at the temples, very distinguished looking. And either inebriated or pissed at his wife.

Dalton caught Cassie's eye. She wasn't happy.

"Grant." Dalton extended his hand and moved toward the guy when it appeared he wasn't going to budge. "Been here long?"

He gave Dalton a firm shake. "This time or the first time?"

Dalton just kind of grunted.

"Next." Mary Jane was just too damn perky.

"I'm Kathy, and this is my husband, Tom." A pretty strawberry blonde with big blue eyes smiled shyly. "We're from Austin, and this is our first time here."

"Nice to meet you both," Cassie said. "It's our first time, too."

"And last," Dalton added, which got Tom's attention.

The guy nodded his blond head in agreement, his narrow tanned face pinched in disgust. Even sitting down he looked tall and lanky. It wasn't just the championship rodeo buckle he wore, or the worn cowboy boots, but the guy looked like a bona fide cowboy. Interestingly, his wife looked and smelled of money. A perfect target for Bask.

"I'm Harvey," the man sitting beside Simone announced, "and that is my wife Zelda." He actually stood and approached Dalton with his hand extended, his expression formal, as if this were a business meeting. "We just got here yesterday."

The guy had a weak grip, which always annoyed Dalton. He smiled at Zelda. In her mid-fifties, she looked to be a good ten years older than Harvey. Or maybe it was just the old-fashioned hairstyle she wore, one thick black braid wrapped around the crown of her head. A liberal sprinkling of gray contributed further to an older appearance.

Zelda smiled back and then took a sip of whatever was in her brandy snifter. A large diamond that had to be at least five carats flashed on her ring finger.

"Well, now that we all know each other a little, let's all just mingle before dinner." Mary Jane planted herself at the bar and started pouring more drinks.

"Where's Robert? I thought he'd be here tonight," Simone asked with that practiced pout.

"Mr. Blankenship had a social engagement tonight. He'll be here first thing in the morning. In plenty of time for your group session."

"Uh, group session?" Dalton glanced from Mary Jane to the others. Tom looked as pleased as Dalton.

Mary Jane tilted her head to the side and in a teasingly scolding tone, she asked, "Didn't you read the week's activity sheet I left in your room?"

"Apparently not." Maybe Cassie was right. Maybe there was a little more swing to this encounter group than he'd expected. He met her widening eyes, and they both asked at the same time, "What group session?"

Mary Jane laughed. "I'm not sure what you two are thinking, but all we do is sit around and discuss general attitudes about marriage, and then we get down to specifics about each couple."

"I know exactly what they're thinking," Simone said with a predatory smile, "and it would be infinitely more fun."

"For God's sake, give it a rest, Simone." Grant drained his drink.

"What's the matter, dear? Afraid you won't measure up?" Simone looked directly at Dalton and blatantly sized him up, and then smiled again.

Grant drew everyone's attention with a few choice words for his wife. Cassie leaned closer to Dalton and chuckling, she said, "Looks like you passed the test, big boy."

"So did you."

She drew back, frowning in her confusion.

He kept his gaze level with hers. "Harvey looks like he's ready to eat you alive," he explained.

She swung her head around to look at the older man. He winked at her.

It was Dalton's turn to chuckle. "Smooth, Cassie, really smooth."

"Shut up, Styles."

"Don't call me that," he whispered. "You're supposed to be my wife."

"No one heard." She sipped the sherry Mary Jane had given her and made a face. "This stuff is nasty."

"Come on. Let's get a real drink and then go for a walk outside."

"We can't just leave now. This is supposed to be the social hour."

"I don't think anyone will miss us." He motioned with his chin. Zelda and Kathy just sat there looking miserable, while Simone held center stage with the men. Except her husband. He stayed near the bar scowling as he worked on his scotch.

"I can see this is going to be a terrific week." Cassie gave him a wry look. "What's really scary is that you're starting to look good."

"Keep it up and all this sweet talk is going to go to my head. Come on." He grabbed her hand. Miraculously she didn't balk, and he skipped the bar and guided them out the sliding glass doors into the garden.

Cassie set down her sherry on one of the patio tables and they took the stone path flanked by fragrant rose bushes with yellow and pink blooms.

"Mary Jane will probably follow us." Cassie led the way, which didn't bother Dalton one bit.

"Let her," he said, enjoying the gentle sway of Cassie's hips, the way her jeans snuggly cupped her rounded backside.

"We'll have to be careful."

"That goes without saying, but if we find a place out in the open, we'll be able to see anyone coming."

"I think we might be headed in the direction of the pool. There'll be a good place to sit there. It's wide-open."

"Good thinking."

She gave him a quick smile over her shoulder that got him wondering about her, about the way she responded to even the slightest praise about her work. Someone had apparently done a number on her in the self-esteem department. Which was ridiculous. He liked to tease her but could see she was pretty and bright and gutsy. A lot of women would have refused to help him with this case. Not Cassie. She'd jumped in with both feet.

They wound through a maze of white daisies and red geraniums and ended up at the large gazebo near the pool's diving board. Constructed of intricate white lattice and stocked with a bar, the gazebo could comfortably seat six people.

Cassie, walking a foot ahead of him, passed it up and headed for a chaise longue. He'd have done the same but he doubted for the same reason.

"Don't you think it would have been more comfortable in the gazebo?" he asked as they both settled in their respective chairs.

"Probably, and I doubt it's bugged, but I figure it's

safer to be out here.'' She stretched out on the chaise, her tummy nice and flat, her breasts round and high.

He felt a tug at his groin. ''Yeah, good thinking.''

There was that pleased smile again. ''I'm starting to worry about this place.''

''You think it's an orgy waiting to happen.''

''If Simone had her way. And Zelda's husband. Can you believe that?''

''Because he has the good taste to find you attractive?''

She blinked, and then looked away as her cheeks turned pink. ''He was the one chasing Simone when we arrived earlier.''

''Really?''

''Yes. Didn't you recognize him?''

''I wasn't exactly looking at *him*.''

Cassie sighed. ''I guess not.''

''Not that Simone's anything to look at, but I was startled.''

''Yeah, right.''

''What?''

She glanced heavenward. ''Not that Simone's anything to look at? Please.''

''She's okay.'' He shrugged. ''Just not my type.''

Cassie looked as if she wanted to say something more but kept her mouth shut.

''So what do you think?'' he asked finally.

''About?''

''This whole situation. These couples all fit the bill. One or both of the spouses have money. The women are all wearing rocks on their fingers. Simone's diamond earrings probably cost more than my car.''

''I noticed. What do you think the story is with Kathy and Tom? They're the oddest pair of the bunch.''

''My guess is that Daddy owns the big ranch worth millions and Tom was one of the hands. He loves her but isn't comfortable having a rich wife. He wants to be the one to take care of her. Thus, their problems.''

Cassie wrinkled her nose. ''That's so old-fashioned.''

''A man wanting to be able to take care of his wife?''

''What difference does it make where the money comes from?''

Dalton shook his head. Some women just didn't get it. Like Linda...his ex thought marriage should be all fun and games. She didn't understand a man's need to prove his worth, to know he could provide for his family no matter what. ''It makes a big difference, trust me.''

''How?''

''Didn't you pay attention to your history lessons?''

Cassie laughed, which really annoyed him. ''I can't wait to hear this explanation.''

''Let's get back to the present problem.'' Dalton was in no mood to spar with any of her feminist notions. ''I'm going to need some time to snoop around. Tonight might be good since we know Bask isn't here.''

She studied him curiously, her gaze probing and irritating. "You feel strongly about a man being head of the household, don't you?"

"It's not about that. Look, don't get off track. Tonight after dinner, see if you can get Mary Jane to show you more of the house. Tell her you used to be an interior decorator, or that you're interested in nineteenth-century houses, whatever."

"And what will you be doing?"

"I'll go with you, just to get more of a feel for the place, but then I'll excuse myself and you keep her busy. I have a feeling the others will be too busy to notice."

"Yeah, either smashed or playing footsies."

He smiled. It was kind of cute when she sounded more Southern.

"What?"

He shrugged. "I agree."

"What's that grin for?"

"Have you lived in Texas all your life?"

She nodded tentatively, looking as if she thought it was a trick question.

"I like your accent."

"Oh." She moistened her lips. "I don't hear it, of course." After a brief hesitation, she said, "We still have to talk about tonight."

"We just did."

"I mean, *tonight* tonight."

"Tonight." He had no idea what she was talking about.

She made a growling sound. "Don't play dumb. We haven't decided on sleeping arrangements."

"Ah, that tonight."

"You think this is so funny." Cassie adjusted the neckline of her T-shirt. As if that did any good. Her breasts strained against the thin stretchy fabric, driving him crazy. "It's obvious what kind of women you hang around. But I'm not like that."

"Glad it's obvious to somebody." Sighing, he locked his hands behind his head and stared at the sky. Staring at her did him no good. "It's been so long since I've 'hung around' I can't remember."

She gave a startled laugh. "Right."

"I wouldn't lie about a thing like that, honey. Too painful." After a long silence, he glanced at her.

She stared at him with a puzzled frown. "Why?"

It was his turn to laugh.

She blinked, and looked down, her cheeks filling with color. "Sorry. None of my business."

"Hey, I'm flattered you find my state of celibacy so hard to believe." He grinned when she rolled her eyes. "I work a lot. I don't have much time to meet women."

She pursed her lips, appearing to consider the information. "So marriage is out of the question?"

"Been there, done that. It doesn't work."

"You've been married?" Her eyes got huge.

"Yeah, for almost two years. That so hard to believe, too?"

"It's hard to picture you as a married man," she admitted. "Do you have any children?"

He shook his head. "Let's figure out tonight before Mary Jane sends the dogs after us."

Cassie nodded, but he could see she had a whole load of questions. Shit! He didn't want to talk about his personal life, especially not about his failed marriage.

"Frankly," he said. "I think it's ridiculous to worry about sleeping in the same bed."

She folded her arms across her chest and glared.

"Unless you think you'd have trouble keeping your hands off me."

"Yeah, that's it."

He smiled. "If it's any comfort, I don't mix business with pleasure." Her eyes narrowed in suspicion, and he raised his hands, palms out in supplication. "I'm telling you, I don't drink on the job, only enough for show, and I don't screw around. It's a distraction I can't afford."

"Oh, well, okay."

Damn, she looked a little disappointed. Dalton shifted in his seat, his blood starting to migrate south. Maybe he should point out that after the week was over they could boink like bunnies. Nah, being that blatant would piss her off.

"So, that's settled. Nobody has to take the floor."

She chewed her lower lip with misgiving. "We'll at least try it tonight."

"Fair enough. I'll try to remember to at least keep my boxers on."

Her jaw slackened, her lips parting in indignation.

He laughed. "Kidding."

A noise came from the shrubbery behind them. Cassie jerked upright. Dalton swung his gaze around. The leaves rattled as if someone or something moved the branches.

Dalton started to get up to investigate when a short Oriental man with a brown weathered face and toothy grin stepped out of the bushes. He stomped debris off his boots at the edge of the pool deck and then gave them a slight bow before he walked toward the path leading to the house.

Cassie pushed off the chaise. "Who the heck is that?"

"I have no idea." Dalton stood, as well, as did the hair at the back of his neck. "I'd like to know how much he heard."

6

"THERE YOU ARE." Mary Jane put her hands on her hips. "I was about to go look for you two."

Cassie forced a smile. "We just went for a walk."

"Private time is good. We encourage it." Mary Jane had changed into a short sleeveless white dress that showed off her tanned legs and arms and plenty of cleavage. "But it is dinnertime and we like to be punctual so the cook can go home."

Cassie caught Dalton's eye just as she was about to inform the other woman that this wasn't kindergarten, and ask her if she knew how to buy the right size bra. The way she busted out all over the place made Cassie cringe.

Dalton didn't seem to mind, although Cassie would give him an A for effort. He tried so hard to keep his gaze above Mary Jane's shoulders that he looked like a robot.

"So there's a chef here, huh?" Dalton gave the other woman one of those heart-stopping smiles. "You look like a woman of many talents. I thought maybe you did the cooking, too."

Mary Jane giggled and linked an arm with Dalton and started toward the dining room. Obviously she wasn't immune to the smile, either, which really ticked Cassie off. It shouldn't, but it did. After all, he was supposed to be acting like her husband.

"If I had to cook, you'd be eating nothing but yogurt and cottage cheese." Mary Jane glanced over her shoulder as if Cassie were an afterthought. "Shall we go? Everyone else is seated for dinner."

"I'm right behind you." Cassie didn't even try to fake a smile. She stared after the two of them, wanting very much to kick Mary Jane's perfect little butt. Wasn't the twit supposed to be helping bring couples together?

And Dalton. He was worse. Great husband, he made.

"So tell me, this cook, does he or she make all the meals?" Dalton asked.

"Yes, Tasha is Russian and doesn't speak much English, but she's a terrific cook. And pastries. You'll love all of her pastries."

Cassie came up alongside them in time to see Mary Jane pat Dalton's stomach.

"Ooh. You can eat all you want and not have to worry one bit." She gave Cassie a smile. "We have a treadmill in the exercise room you can use."

Cassie blinked in astonishment. Had she just been insulted? Mary Jane looked so innocent, yet...

The startled amusement on Dalton's face cinched it. He turned his head, and she knew it was to keep from laughing. Cassie pried his arm away from Mary Jane. "Excuse me, but I'd like to speak to my husband. Alone."

"But dinner…" She gestured to the open dining room. Everyone was already seated and looking at them.

"Tough" teetered on Cassie's tongue. "Go ahead. We'll be there in a moment."

"Oh." Mary Jane cast a helpless glance at the others. "Okay, but I'm going to let Tasha start serving."

"Good idea." Cassie took the arm she'd absconded and steered Dalton down the hall a few yards.

"I'm flattered that you're jealous but what the hell are you doing? I was trying to find out about the guy outside."

"He's the gardener. I saw him carrying rakes and a leaf blower to an old pickup."

"I kind of figured, but that doesn't mean we're in the clear."

"I didn't think we were, but I bet he doesn't speak much if any English. The cook is Russian? Please. How many people speak Japanese or Russian around here?" She glanced over her shoulder to make sure no one had approached. "Sounds like they're covering their tracks both ways. The staff doesn't understand and the guests can't talk to them."

Dalton stared at her, the corners of his mouth beginning to lift. Warmth flooded her. The look of approval he gave her made her knees weaker than his sexy smile did.

"Nice deduction, Cassie."

She lifted a shoulder in a nonchalant shrug even though her heart pounded like crazy. "I'll ask Mary

Jane some gardening questions and get around to finding out how much English the gardener knows.''

He held her wrist when she started to leave. ''What
did you bring me out here for? Was that it?''

''I—yes, I think so. I don't really remember.''

''You know that when I pay attention to Mary Jane
it's all acting.''

''Why would I care that you pay attention to her?
Or if you were seriously interested?''

''We have to appear vulnerable so that Robert ap-
proaches you.''

''This conversation is totally unnecessary.'' She
tried to twist out of his hold.

''Wait. The thing is, it would be better if you didn't
act jealous.''

She gasped. ''I'm not acting jealous.''

His eyebrows rose. ''It's not an act?''

''You know what I mean.''

He smiled. ''If it looks like you don't care who I
sniff around, Bask will think you're easy pickings.''

''Sniff around? What a charming way to put it.''

A sheepish look briefly crossed his face. ''It
wouldn't hurt if you did a little flirting yourself.''

''These men are all married.''

''I said flirt, not jump their bones.''

''You really need to work on your vocabulary.''

''Hey, you two.'' Mary Jane's voice startled them.
She'd poked her head out of the dining room. ''We're
waiting dinner on you.''

''Sorry,'' Cassie muttered and exchanged one last

look with Dalton before leading the way back down the hall.

"Have you two been arguing?" Mary Jane asked as they all sat down at the table.

Mary Jane gestured Dalton to the empty seat beside her, so Cassie took the only other available chair next to Harvey. The way he grinned at her made her skin crawl.

"Nope." Dalton smiled. "I'm a lover not a fighter."

Cassie rolled her gaze heavenward.

Mary Jane giggled. "Good. You all are supposed to be reconnecting, not arguing."

"I'm ready to do some connecting," Harvey said to no one in particular, and Cassie felt something hit her leg.

Pretty sure it was Harvey's hand, she shifted her knees in the other direction.

"Yes, Harvey, we all know about you," Simone said in a bored voice. "I need another martini."

"Tasha will be bringing in the soup at any moment. Ah, here she is."

A short, stocky dark-haired woman with thick nylons and black shoes that resembled combat boots came through the swinging doors carrying a large ceramic tureen. Her gruff expression didn't waver as she set the soup on the buffet against the wall.

"I don't want any soup. I want a martini. Grant?" Simone gave her husband an expectant look.

"We're going to have wine in a minute, Simone, just hold on."

She stiffened, her gaze throwing daggers at her husband. "I don't want to have to ask you again."

Silence saturated the room while the couple dueled with their eyes. Finally, Grant muttered a curse and got up from the table and headed for the parlor.

Tasha paid no attention. She ladled what looked like a borsht into bowls and set one before each person.

"Simone." Mary Jane's voice was surprisingly stern.

"You're not a rookie at this. You know better. This is not the way to start off the week."

"Shut up, Mary Jane. Easy for you to say. It's obvious you already have designs on him." She glanced at Dalton and then drained the last few drops of her martini.

Mary Jane turned redder than a tomato. "Simone, I think perhaps you've had enough to drink."

The older woman looked as if she were about to bite off Mary Jane's head, but then backed off and stared at her plate.

Odd. Really odd. Cassie had missed something. She'd have made a sizable bet that Simone would never have deferred to the younger woman. Dalton seemed a little puzzled, too, so at least it wasn't her imagination.

Mary Jane smiled brightly at the others. "You're going to love this cabbage soup. It's a borsht, kind of sweet and sour. It's a favorite here."

While Tasha finished serving, the silence grew thick and awkward. Cassie seized the moment. "Mary Jane,

I noticed there are some Brigadoon roses out by the pool."

The other woman wrinkled her nose. "I don't know anything about flowers."

"Oh, I had a question about them. You have a gardener, I assume?"

"Mr. Hamada comes three days a week, but I'm afraid he doesn't speak English."

Cassie sighed, forcing herself not to look at Dalton. "Oh, too bad."

"Is that really cabbage?" Tom's tone of disgust drew everyone's attention. "Why is it a funny color?"

"Tom." Kathy laid a hand on her husband's arm.

He made a face at the soup again, but said nothing more.

Grant returned with Simone's drink and she smiled up at him as she took the glass. "You need to take lessons from Tom here. He knows when to shut up."

Mary Jane reached across Dalton and grabbed the martini, splashing some of it on the white tablecloth. "Enough, Simone." She gave the other woman a pointed glare, and then returned to a perky smile. "Okay, everyone has their soup. Let's eat."

The silence grew awkward again, while everyone concentrated on their food until Harvey suggested Mary Jane fill them in on tomorrow's activities.

She demurred at first. "I thought I'd wait until dessert."

"Why? Most of us know what we're in for." Harvey gave Cassie another one of those skin-prickling grins. "Maybe I should explain."

"That's all right." Mary Jane quickly set down her spoon. "As most of you know, tomorrow morning we meet for our group session where we'll discuss what we hope to accomplish during this next week."

Simone laughed. "I don't think that's the part Harvey is interested in."

Mary Jane gave her a warning glance. "At that time you'll discuss issues in the marriage that have been the cause of disagreements. Every person will have the floor without any interruption, and then your spouse will have a chance to respond. Later, we'll discuss observations of the others about how each couple communicates."

Great. Cassie looked at Dalton. Her only consolation was that he didn't look any more thrilled over the exercise than she was.

"After lunch," Mary Jane continued, "you'll relearn how to touch each other."

Cassie was damn glad she didn't have anything in her mouth that she could've spit out.

"Now, we're talking," Harvey said, and brushed up against Cassie's leg.

She had a good mind to give him a bruising pinch that would remind him to keep his hands to himself for the rest of the week. Dalton caught her eye and the concern in his face warmed her. He couldn't possibly have seen Harvey's deliberate touch but something in her expression must have alerted him. She gave him a reassuring smile, and he winked.

Silly how the small gesture turned her to mush. Ridiculous, really, but it seemed so personal, as if she was the only one in the room with him, as if they shared some private joke or secret. Which of course they did, making her reaction all the more silly.

Mary Jane directed her smile at Cassie and Tom and Kathy. "Don't pay attention to them. They like riling the newcomers. It's their version of an initiation."

Tom and Kathy exchanged nervous glances.

"Tomorrow afternoon you'll relearn how to touch each other," Mary Jane said evenly. "The exercise will start with massage class."

Tom muttered a curse.

Kathy coughed. "In front of everyone?"

"Only during the massage lesson. I'll show you the Swedish version and make sure you're doing it correctly. After that, you'll break up and practice in private. I'll peek in from time to time to make sure you're staying in the spirit of the exercise."

Cassie held her breath. This was not what she'd signed up for. She didn't want to touch Dalton. Well, she did, but that was the problem.

Dalton laughed, and everyone stared at him. "Explain this spirit of the exercise."

"Pleasing your partner."

"Oh, goody." Simone had managed to recover her martini and she sipped it with a bored expression. "How about if we want to please someone else's—"

"The goal," Mary Jane quickly continued, effectively cutting off Simone, "is to recapture the feelings you had when you first met, when you began dating and wanted nothing more than to please each other."

Simone let out a bored sigh. "Well, Grant, it looks as if we missed a phase."

Her husband didn't so much as blink.

"When you say you'll be peeking in, do you mean into our rooms?" Cassie asked, and Tom and Kathy leaned forward with interest.

"Wherever you choose to give the massages. By the pool, or in the exercise room, your bedroom, it's up to you."

At the mention of public places, Cassie breathed with relief. The session couldn't be too bad.

Mary Jane picked up the brass bell in front of her plate and rang for Tasha. "Of course most couples choose the privacy of their rooms since we encourage nudity."

DALTON SLIPPED into Bask's office and locked the door behind him. A computer sat on the credenza behind a large teak desk, already on, but dormant. He moved the mouse, and then while he waited for the computer to come to life, he checked the desk drawers. No luck. Bask had locked everything tight. Dalton would have to break in later. Right now, the information in the computer interested him more.

A couple of file folders sat on the corner of the desk.

He rifled through them. Nothing of particular note, but he copied some names and phone numbers of potential clients. Or maybe they were former clients. Either way, the information could prove useful.

Several icons appeared on the computer screen and he sat down to study them. The chair creaked under his weight, and his gaze flew toward the door. He waited a couple of minutes. No light came on in the hall.

Damn, he should have used Cassie as a lookout or distraction. He laughed to himself. That was the problem. She was already a distraction. What the hell was wrong with him anyway? Spending the week together posing as husband and wife, sharing the same room—shit, the same bed—how could he have thought otherwise?

Her scent alone was enough to drive him crazy. Sweet and sexy and sinful all at once. Man, he had to stay on guard every minute, really focus or he was going to blow this fluff case. Talk about getting egg on his face.

He checked out the directory and went to the database program, although Bask would be an idiot to leave evidence there. Which didn't mean there wouldn't be clues. He found some more names and addresses, and downloaded the files into the disk he'd brought with him. Then he looked for correspondence. By the time he'd read the first several, he realized they were all form letters, and the names on them were the same ones in the database.

One final check for anything in the word processing program and then he had to get out of Dodge. But before he did, he made sure he erased his trail. No need to take any more risks than he already had.

CASSIE BOLTED upright as soon as she heard Dalton slip into the room. ''Where the hell have you been?''

"Miss me?"

"I thought you'd only be gone a—" She cut herself off, remembering she had to keep her voice lowered.

Dalton didn't seem concerned. As if they'd shared a room a hundred times before, he unbuttoned his shirt and shrugged out of it. She'd left the bathroom light on with the door opened a crack, enough for light to filter into the bedroom but not broadcast the fact that they were still awake.

Dalton stood directly in the path of the illumination, his bare chest in full view. "I made some headway. Not much, but some."

"Did you—?" She stopped herself, frustrated that they couldn't talk freely.

"Hold on. I'll get into bed in a minute." He scratched his bare chest and shoved a hand through his hair.

He looked tired. And maddeningly sexy with the light sprinkling of hair that arrowed toward his waist. His skin was a golden tan all the way to the top of his low-riding jeans. He removed his belt and she shifted her gaze when her thoughts began to falter. She plumped her pillow, but out of the corner of her eye tracked his movement to the bathroom.

He opened the door wide, letting light flood over her and she automatically pulled the sheets up to cover her breasts, which was ridiculous since she had her bra on under her nightshirt.

He left the door partially open while he brushed his teeth and washed his face. She'd seen a pair of shorts draped over his suitcase and wondered if that was what he'd sleep in.

"You want the light left on?" he asked a few minutes later, standing in the doorway, watching her, his hand on the switch.

"No, thanks." Her mouth had grown dry and her pulse speeded up, but not because she was anxious for him to get in bed. Well, she was, but only so they could talk. She tugged down her shirt even though she wore shorts beneath.

He flipped the switch and the sudden darkness blinded her.

"Ouch! Dammit."

"What's wrong?" She blinked, trying to get her eyes to adjust.

"I hit my toe on the corner of the bed."

"You could've left the light on if you wanted."

"Dammit."

"What now?"

"I hit the other corner."

Cassie laughed, but then the mattress dipped with his weight and she couldn't remember what was so funny.

"I'm glad my pain entertains you," he said, his voice awfully close.

"Pain? You stubbed your toe."

"Like that's supposed to tickle?"

"Oh, poor baby." Her eyes had adjusted and she was able to see his outline. As far as she knew he hadn't changed from his jeans. He couldn't possibly have. Was that what he planned on sleeping in?

"Come on. I know you want me in perfect shape for tomorrow."

"Yeah, that's it," she said with as much sarcasm as she could muster, considering her stomach turned somersaults at the reminder of their massage lesson.

He chuckled so close the vibration tickled her ear. She stiffened, afraid to breathe. How had he managed to get that close?

"Cassie?"

"Yeah?"

"You're not going to get all prim and modest on me tomorrow, are you?"

"What's wrong with being prim and modest? I bet Kathy won't be too anxious to strip down and let us watch her get massaged."

"But you're not the type." His voice was so low she had to move her head closer to hear him.

"I beg your pardon."

"Don't get all offended. I only meant that most pretty women with a body like yours like to show off their goods."

She didn't say anything, too overwhelmed by a mix of embarrassment and pleasure.

"Ah, hell, you know what I mean." He sighed loudly. "Why don't you get some sleep. We'll talk tomorrow."

"No way." She quickly summoned her composure. "I want to know what you found tonight."

"Nothing incriminating in itself. His office was a piece of cake to get into and I managed to get into his computer and download some client names."

"Is what you're doing legal?"

A flash of teeth told her he was smiling. "As I was saying, the names might help us in case we need corroborating witnesses. Also some bank names but no account numbers. Even here he's cautious."

"Anything else?"

"A plane ticket to Rio."

"Well, that's something. For when?"

"That I didn't get."

"But that's important. That'll tell us when he's planning on closing a deal."

"No kidding, Sherlock. I heard someone in the hall and had to turn the light off."

Stung by his remark, she bit her lower lip.

"Cassie." He touched her cheek. "I'm sorry. I'm tired and disappointed I didn't find more, but I have no business taking it out on you."

"No big deal."

His fingers trailed her cheek to her hairline. He paused and then plunged them into her hair. "Without him here, tonight was the perfect opportunity to get something on him, and I blew it."

"No, you didn't. If there was nothing to get what could you do?" She closed her eyes, enjoying the way he massaged her scalp and then worked his way to the back of her neck. "Don't be so hard on yourself."

"Yeah, you're right. But now I'll have to poke around while he's here."

"You mean, we."

"Right. Now we hope he makes a move on you soon."

"Great." She shifted, uncomfortable suddenly at the thought of getting cozy with Bask, and accidentally hit Dalton's with her foot. His leg. Briefly. But enough to know it was bare. But how? He'd had on jeans. His shorts were in the closet....

Oh, God.

"We're the most likely target. It's pretty obvious you can't stand me and you want out."

"Huh?" Dare she touch his leg again? Just to make sure it was really bare. His words finally registered. "That's not true."

"Here you go getting defensive again. It should look like we've about had it with each other."

"Simone and Grant look like far more likely candidates. They've gone beyond despising each other to indifference. Nothing worse than that."

Dalton remained silent for a long time. He moved away from her and rolled onto his back. "Let's get some sleep."

She'd obviously said something wrong. But what? They were talking about the case. Or had she somehow struck close to home for him? "Dalton?"

"Yeah?"

She started to touch his shoulder but pulled back. Ever since he'd told her he didn't mix business with pleasure, the thought of kissing him, lying naked beside him, simmered in the back of her mind. Had that been his ploy? "Good night."

"Good night, Cassie." He turned over, giving her his back.

7

"I'M NEVER GOING to be like your daddy, Kathy. You knew that when you married me." Tom folded his arms across his chest, his expression dark and mutinous.

Two feet away facing him, Kathy leaned forward in her metal folding chair. "I'm not asking you to be like him. That's not what I want. I just want you to give him a chance. He offered you a job because of your ability, not because you're my husband."

"I'm happy riding the rodeo circuit."

"You can't do it forever. You've already broken both legs and dislocated your shoulder, and next month you'll be thirty-two."

He gave a harsh sigh. "Quit trying to make me into something I'm not."

Kathy's eyes filled with tears. "I'm not. I just don't want you to get hurt. I want to grow old with you."

Cassie sniffed. It was difficult to watch. Simone and Grant had already had their turn but the only feeling they inspired in Cassie was annoyance. She wanted to give each of them a swift kick.

Kathy and Tom were a different matter. Cassie's heart ached for them. They obviously loved each other, but sadly, money and pride were getting in the way of their relationship.

"Hey," Dalton said quietly, reaching for her hand. "You okay?"

She nodded quickly and felt a tear slip down her cheek. She dabbed it away, unaware she'd gotten misty-eyed. God, how embarrassing. She chanced a peek at Dalton. He had such a tender, sympathetic expression it made her want to weep.

He leaned closer to her. "Maybe this is what Tom and Kathy need. Better to air out their feelings than to blindside each other later."

"I know. I just wish they had qualified counselors helping them."

"When this is over, how about we make sure they get it?" he whispered.

Surprised, Cassie turned to him. His mouth was just inches from hers. His breath touched her lips. "That would be great."

He smiled. "You realize we're up next."

"Yup."

"I'm not looking forward to it either." His gaze went to Bask who sat to the right, facing the couple, with a notebook on his lap.

He had all the moves down, from the concerned expression to the intermittent scribble of notes. Cassie couldn't think of anyone she despised more. The way he played with people's lives for profit. The reminder helped her get in the acting mode.

At Dalton's suggestion, they'd decided to ad-lib. Cassie only hoped there wouldn't be a lot of long silent moments. She turned her attention back to Tom and Kathy, warmed by Dalton's suggestion that they steer the couple toward a legitimate counselor.

Every once in a while she saw a soft side to him that made her melt. Like the way he'd paid special attention to Zelda at breakfast when Harvey had acted like a jackass toward her, or when he'd carried the heavy dinner tray into the kitchen for Tasha last night.

He certainly had his good qualities. But she was better off not thinking about those right now. She checked her watch. In five minutes, Tom and Kathy would be finished, and it would be her and Dalton's turn to air their dirty laundry.

Tom and Kathy wrapped up their session with tears and kisses, and an appointment for private counseling with Bask. The thought of the two of them, vulnerable and desperate, opening up to the sleazeball made Cassie's blood boil.

"Okay." Bask stood and faced the audience as Tom and Kathy reclaimed their seats beside Cassie.

Impulsively she leaned over and squeezed Kathy's hand. The other woman smiled shyly and squeezed back.

"I think that went quite well." Bask's oily smile had Cassie clenching her teeth. "We all have a feel for the difficulties facing Tom and Kathy. As the week goes on, you'll all be able to contribute your observations. Now, we'll hear from Dalton and Cassie."

Cassie hesitated. She didn't get up until Dalton stood and offered her a hand. Her knees went a little weak and she kind of hobbled alongside him toward the two chairs vacated by Tom and Kathy.

She knew she looked nervous, but that was okay. Everyone else had appeared the same way except for Simone. As usual she simply looked bored.

As soon as they were seated and facing each other, Cassie realized that Dalton wasn't thrilled to be up there either. In fact, he seemed pretty agitated. That surprised her. He'd been relatively calm until now.

"All right, let's see." Bask frowned. "Who should go first?"

They exchanged looks, neither of them offering.

"I think Dalton should go first," Simone said, showing the first sign of interest all morning.

Bask nodded. "If that's okay with you two, let's get started." He reclaimed his seat and picked up his notebook and pen.

Dalton cleared his throat, pushed his fingers through his hair. "You all should know I didn't want to come here." He glared at Cassie. "I'm being blackmailed into it."

"Address your wife, not us," Bask said.

Dalton exhaled sharply. "I think the marriage is just fine. I do what I'm supposed to do. Work hard. Make a living. Prepare for a family..."

What is he doing? Cassie thought frantically. He was blowing it. Cassie stared him in the eyes, trying to get him to wake up. *We're supposed to be rich, not hardworking!*

"Yeah, it takes time and energy. That doesn't mean I love her any less—"

"Dalton." Bask drew his attention. "Remember to address Cassie. Don't speak about her like she's not here."

Dalton frowned, and looked confused for a moment. "Right." He glanced at the others, and then focused on Cassie. And said nothing.

"Try to relax," Bask said. "Expressing your feelings doesn't mean you're right or wrong. Remember, you're fighting to save your marriage. Let it all out."

"Shit! I don't want to do this." Dalton stood suddenly, nearly knocking over his chair.

"Dalton." Taken aback, Cassie didn't know what to say at first. If she didn't know better, she wouldn't believe he was acting. She touched his hand. It was clammy. "You promised, honey," she said, holding his gaze captive.

He stared back for a long silent moment and then sat down again. "Okay." He took a deep breath that made his chest visibly rise and fall. "I guess the trouble is, roles are blurred nowadays. Maybe I'm a little old-fashioned but I want to provide for my family. I want—"

"Ha!" Cassie cut him off before he totally blew their cover. "Your mother pays the bills."

"Cassie," Bask interjected in a warning voice. "You'll have your turn."

Dalton straightened. Cassie breathed a silent sigh of relief that Dalton seemed to be back on track. "My trust fund pays the bills, but it's not like I don't work. I have a job, managing our finances and making sure our investments are yielding the highest dividends possible. I dabble in the family business. Hell, I earn my keep.

"You're the one who seems to think life should be all fun and games, that my every waking moment should be centered on you. It doesn't work that way. A man has to prove his worth, provide for his family. All I've ever asked is that you be there for me."

Cassie tried to look bored the way Simone had, but it was hard to ignore the passion with which he spoke. She got the feeling he wasn't acting. The way he fisted his hands and clenched his jaw, the grim expression on his face, it was all pretty unnerving.

"You can't have it both ways, Linda. Either we work as a team or—"

Cassie gasped. Part of it was pure reaction. "Wrong wife," she managed to say.

He frowned, clearly confused. "What?"

"Let's see..." She pursed her lips as if in thought when her heart was ready to leap from her chest. "Was Linda number one or two?"

He paled, and then glanced at the others when someone giggled. "Okay, that's it." He stood, and there was no mistaking the finality in his face. "We're done for today."

"Cassie hasn't had her turn," Bask said calmly.

She quickly stood, too. "If he isn't going to finish I'm not saying a word."

"Suit yourself," Dalton said, and walked out of the room without a backward glance.

EVERYONE TURNED to look at him as he sat down for lunch. He couldn't meet Cassie's eyes. She had to be wondering what the hell had happened to him. He'd already made up a story for when they had some privacy. The truth was, he needed to drive. Alone. Clear his head. Get rid of the old tapes.

Man, he couldn't believe he'd reacted that way. He honestly didn't think about Linda much. They'd been divorced for two years and she'd already remarried. Which had been no surprise. She'd been seeing the guy the last two months of their marriage.

He finally had the guts to meet Cassie's gaze. She looked worried. The others were busy digging into their Caesar salads. Not Simone, though. She watched them with predatory interest.

"After lunch we'll take about an hour break to have showers or naps or whatever." It was obviously Mary Jane's turn to baby-sit. Bask was absent. "Then we'll meet by the pool for our massage instruction."

"Shall we wear swimsuits?" Kathy asked, her nervous gaze darting to her husband.

Mary Jane nodded. "If you like."

"What's the alternative?" Zelda rarely spoke, and turned pink when everyone stared at her.

"Anything that makes you comfortable." Mary Jane smiled. "However, in order to get a proper massage, you will need your back bare."

Zelda openly shuddered. "I don't remember a massage lesson the last time we were here."

"You were sick that day, darling." Harvey picked up her hand and kissed the back of it. "One of your migraines kept you in the room all day."

The tender gesture surprised Dalton. The guy was like a chameleon, a weasel one minute, and charming the next.

Zelda gave him a wan smile. "I guess I could wear a swimsuit."

"That's the spirit." He kissed her hand again and then laid it down on the table, his predatory gaze going immediately to Cassie.

She gave him a dirty look and turned her attention to Mary Jane. "Why out by the pool?" she asked. "That doesn't sound practical."

"Oh, you'll see. We'll be all set up for it."

"I hope we're having more than salad for lunch," Tom said, his plate already clean. "No way is this enough until dinner."

"Tasha will be bringing out some fruit shortly."

Tom made a face. "Fruit?"

Mary Jane gave him a patronizing smile. "You don't want to get too full for this afternoon. Trust me."

Cassie darted Dalton an accusatory glare and then concentrated on her salad. As if he'd orchestrated the afternoon. He wasn't so thrilled about disrobing and getting massaged either.

That was a lie. He was getting hard just thinking about Cassie running her hands over him.

Shit! Not good. Not good at all. He hadn't been kidding about not needing the distraction.

"Here's our dessert now." Mary Jane and her perky attitude was starting to get on his nerves.

Tasha carried in a large glass bowl filled with colorful chunks of melon and grapes and whole strawberries. It looked pretty good but Dalton was with Tom…he wanted real food.

"As soon as you finish, take the hour to relax and do whatever you need to do." Mary Jane had barely gotten the words out of her mouth when Tom and Grant both pushed away from the table.

Grant looked at his watch. "At the pool by one-thirty, right?"

"Well, well, aren't we anxious?" Simone sipped her mimosa. Everyone else had non-alcoholic drinks, but Simone had insisted on the orange juice and champagne.

Grant ignored her and left the dining room with a look of disgust. Dalton decided he'd hate to be on the receiving end of either of their massages. Simone was probably capable of scratching like a wildcat, and half the time Grant looked as if he could cheerfully wring her neck.

What the hell kept those two together? Watching them made him glad he was divorced. At least he and Linda hadn't had time to get to the sniping stage. She'd taken up with their divorced neighbor while Dalton had been in New York on assignment. She complained that he never had enough time for her, and she left. Moved to Seattle. Just like that.

He realized Cassie had gotten up from the table while he'd been lost in thought. The way she stared at him with intense curiosity made him wonder what his expression had revealed. He stood and followed her out of the dining room, leaving the others to chat with Mary Jane.

"You going to the room?" he asked, but she wouldn't turn around. Probably still pissed at him for leaving like he had earlier.

Instead of heading for the stairs, she slipped out the French doors into the garden. He followed close behind and when they got a few yards away from the house, she spun around, her eyes shooting daggers.

"What the hell was that about?" Anger radiated from her.

"Could you be more specific?"

"Damn you."

"I suggest you keep your voice down."

"Ah." Her lips curved in a humorless smile. "You almost blew our cover by spewing garbage about working for a living and needing to provide for a family, and you worry about me raising my voice."

"That isn't garbage," he said quietly.

A thoughtful frown drew her brows together and she studied him more closely. Immediately he regretted his words. They weren't really talking about him, it was all supposed to be an act, and anyway, he didn't want her poking around his personal business.

"Come on, Dalton. What was all that about Linda?"

"Nothing. Why all the questions?"

Her eyebrows rose. "Aren't I supposed to know about my husband? And I might remind you, I wasn't the one who added another layer of back story. So don't get huffy with me." She placed her hands on her hips. "And where did you run off to without telling me?"

"I went to call my ex-partner to run a check on Mary Jane."

"And?"

"She looks clean so far."

"And?" The stubborn glint in her eyes told him he wasn't going to get off that easy.

"All right already." He muttered a curse. She was getting the wife role down a little too pat. "Yes, Linda is my ex-wife. We've been divorced for two years."

"Any kids?"

"God, no."

She frowned. "You don't like children."

"I love kids. I'm just glad we didn't have any to drag through a divorce."

"Nasty, huh?"

"Not really." Man, he did not want to talk about this. His ego had been bruised enough.

"What happened?"

"That you don't need to know."

Cassie made a face. "So long as you don't spring any more surprises on me."

He sighed. "One day I came home from an assignment and she basically said 'see ya,' and that was that."

Cassie gasped. "How awful."

He shrugged. "Meant to be, I guess. Someone in my profession has no business getting married anyway."

"You don't believe that."

"Why not? I'm living proof, aren't I?"

"Marriages go bad for a lot of different reasons.

Why are you so willing to accept the blame because of your job?''

"Look, not that I don't appreciate your concern, but save the psychoanalysis for the others." Shit, he wouldn't have followed her out here if he knew she was going to start digging into his personal life.

Cassie wasn't fooled by his attempt at nonchalance. He'd been hurt by the breakup of his marriage. It was in his face, and clearly in the way he'd reacted this morning. The thought that he might still love his ex-wife made Cassie a little melancholy. She didn't know why. It just did.

"Okay," she said finally, "we don't have to talk about it anymore. Just don't spring any surprises on me. Deal?"

He winced. "This morning wasn't kosher. I apologize for that." Something caught his attention behind her. He frowned and she started to turn around when he said, "Kiss me."

"What?"

"Just kiss me, dammit."

No chance to respond after that. He pulled her roughly against him and used one hand to hold her by the back of the neck while he pressed his lips to hers. She couldn't catch her breath and tried to break away.

"Bask." Dalton broke contact long enough to murmur, "He's headed toward us."

This time when he kissed her she responded, kissing him back, teasing him with her tongue across his lips. He made a low growling sound and plunged inside her mouth. Her breath faltered and she sank heavily against him when his hands roamed her back and then dug into the curve of her buttocks.

"Looks as if this morning's session wasn't a total waste." Bask's amused voice cut through the haze.

Slowly they parted. Dalton looked as dazed as she felt.

"I didn't mean to interrupt." Bask sidestepped them on the path, motioning with his hand. "Please, continue."

Cassie smiled sheepishly, her heart racing out of control. They waited until Bask was a good ways down the path and out of earshot before they even looked at each other.

"Well, we blew that." Cassie's hand shook as she shoved the hair out of her face, and she quickly lowered it.

He narrowed his gaze. "How so?"

"We're supposed to be disgusted with each other and now it looks as if we were hiding in the garden making out."

"So? That's the way married life works. You fight and make up, fight and make up. You don't necessarily have to be getting along."

Cassie made a face. Was he teasing? "That doesn't sound very enticing at all."

Amusement lifted one side of his mouth. "You think it should be all bliss? The white picket fence. Dinner together every night at six."

She thought for a moment. "No, those things don't have anything to do with a marriage. They're external aspects. Marriage is more about friendship and loyalty and support and, of course, love.''

The way he looked at her with such odd intensity made her uncomfortable. Did he think she was being sappy? She didn't care. Better than being cynical.

''You asked,'' she said in her own defense. ''So what if I've never been married. That's what I want, and I won't settle for less. Even if I end up being a spinster.''

A slow smile lifted his lips. ''A spinster? I haven't heard that term in a while.''

''Make fun of me. I don't care.''

The smile vanished. ''I'm not making fun of you. I hope you find someone to give you all those things. You're right, a marriage should be about friendship and love. It just doesn't usually work out that way.''

''I'll buy that it doesn't always work out that way, but not usually. I know a lot of very happy couples.''

''With nine-to-five jobs and a house in the suburbs.''

''Wrong, but you don't want to believe me, so I'm not going to waste my breath.'' Her gaze went to his mouth and she instantly remembered the kiss they shared minutes ago.

As if he could read her mind, he said, ''You forgot to add sexual attraction to the marriage list.''

''No, I didn't. That goes along with love.''

His left brow lifted in amusement. ''Does it?''

''Of course.''

''I didn't figure you to be naive.''

Annoyance rattled her, and then it occurred to her

he was trying to do just that. "We don't agree, so that makes me naive? Interesting tactic."

"Tactic? Where did that come from? I'm just going with the flow."

She gave him a smug smile. "Of course."

He met her challenge with a squinty stare. Before she knew it, he grabbed both her wrists and hauled her up against him. He muffled her startled cry with his mouth, kissing her hard, slipping his tongue between her lips and sweeping the inside of her mouth.

She resisted at first, but her heart pounded with excitement, her knees so weak she thought she might slide to the ground if he released her. She wiggled her wrists free and wound her arms around his neck. He didn't relent. He tasted and teased, and his erection, hard and heavy, nudged her tummy.

Dampness gathered between her thighs. The heady fragrance of roses clouded her senses. This is what she'd wanted, what she'd lain in bed thinking about long into the night. She wanted to touch him, be touched by him. Lie naked beside him in bed.

Gently he cupped one breast through her T-shirt, running his finger over the nipple until it was so hard and extended she thought she'd burst if he didn't take it into his mouth. Even the slightest brush with his fingers made her quiver. Electric heat, urgent, pressing, made it hard to think.

She took one arm from around his neck and pressed her palm against his chest. Slowly she dragged her hand down his chest to his belly, anxious to feel the length of his shaft. She got to his belt buckle, and he pulled back, leaving her startled and embarrassed.

She straightened and looked at him through glazed eyes as she tried to find her equilibrium.

His chest heaved with his ragged breathing. "Are you going to deny you enjoyed that as much as I did?"

She stared mutely at him, confused by his sudden withdrawal, his question, the challenge in his voice.

"Answer me."

"Of course I won't deny it. My reaction was pretty obvious." Resentment and anger built inside her. "What kind of game are you playing?"

"No game. Simply proving a point."

"You did a hell of a job. I have no idea what you're talking about."

He smiled, apparently unfazed by her growing anger. "You enjoyed the foreplay. I enjoyed it. Given the opportunity we probably would have taken our lust further." She cringed at the word. "That, sweetheart, was all about sex. It didn't have a damn thing to do with love."

8

CASSIE HADN'T BROUGHT a swimsuit. Not that she'd wear one if she had. Shorts and a T-shirt were good enough for the massage lesson. Anything covered didn't need massaging.

She checked her watch and then headed toward the pool area. Maybe she'd luck out and Dalton wouldn't even show. She hadn't seen him for the past forty-five minutes, not since she'd left him in the garden.

The jerk.

She pushed thoughts of him aside. Thinking about him, replaying the scene in the garden would only get her mad again. And when she was mad, she was liable to say something impulsive in front of the others.

Damn him. At least she had the satisfaction of knowing he'd been as turned on as she had been. He couldn't have faked an erection like the one that had pressed hard against her belly, creating such a heat in her she'd feared she'd explode.

Oh, God, she couldn't think about that right now. Not ever. Dalton had made it quite clear he was unavailable. Not that she was interested.

As soon as she got off the garden path, she saw him sitting on a lawn chair near the pool talking to Mary

Jane. He had his shirt off, and Cassie had to take a deep, steadying breath. He had the perfect vee shape, broad shoulders and chest, narrow at the waist and hips. Genetics. It had to be. He couldn't have time to workout. Not him. He was too busy with his job. Too busy for a wife and family.

The idea annoyed her. She wasn't sure why. Maybe because she didn't believe him. But that didn't make his feelings anymore of her business.

As she got closer she realized Mary Jane had on a swimsuit. A very tiny bikini. Of course she had the kind of body that could be totally naked and still look stunning. Tanned and toned and well proportioned. Except for her breasts. Too round and perfect. She had to have had a boob job.

Tempted to swing around the opposite side of the pool and join Zelda, Tom and Kathy, Cassie had to concede when Mary Jane spotted her and waved her over.

"The others should be here any minute and then we can start. You'll need to pick out the scented oil you want to use." She glanced at Dalton, something Cassie tried steadfastly not to do. "I was wondering if you two would like to go first?"

"Sure," Dalton said at the same time Cassie said, "No, thanks."

She laughed. "I'll leave you to discuss it." She got up from the lawn chair and strode across the deck toward the others.

Cassie tried not to gape at the backside view.

Dalton's head leaned to the left as he watched her

walk away, as if he were tying to get as full a view as possible. "That is some thong. How do they work, anyway?"

"How do they work?"

"Yeah." He hadn't taken his eyes off Mary Jane. "I mean, how does that thing feel splitting you in two like that?"

"I have a pair if you want to try it on."

"You do?" He swung his gaze to her, his eyes lit with hope. "How come I haven't seen it?"

"In your dreams."

He laughed. "Yeah." His gaze went back to Mary Jane.

"You're a pig." How could he arouse her so easily one minute, and infuriate her the next?

"You just figure that out?" He shaded his eyes and squinted when she rounded the pool into the path of the sun. "You think she's boinking Bask?"

Cassie stared at him in disbelief. "Grow up."

"What?" He met her gaze, all innocence.

"Of course she is."

This time he laughed loud enough for everyone to turn around and look at them. Ignoring them, he grinned at Cassie. "I can see you're going to keep me on my toes."

"You're amazing, you know that?"

"I like it when a woman tells me I'm amazing."

She shook her head, saddened suddenly. "Why are you doing this?"

"Doing what?"

She stayed stubbornly silent. But even that didn't

seem to faze him. His expression remained unreadable, his stance relaxed with his hands now locked behind his head as he reclined.

After a few minutes, he said, "Don't you want to do this massage thing first and get it over with?"

She sat on the lounge chair Mary Jane had vacated. He hadn't even asked what Cassie had meant. Either he honestly didn't care, or he'd changed the subject on purpose because he didn't want to get into a discussion about why he was acting like such a jerk. Was he purposely trying to push her away?

He sighed. "Are you going to answer or give me the silent treatment?"

She snapped out of her musings and looked at him. "Give you the silent treatment," she said sweetly, and got up to join the others.

"OKAY, ARE WE all comfortable?" Mary Jane flashed her smile around the group, and actually waited until people started nodding.

Dalton lay facedown on the massage table, waiting for Mary Jane to use him in her demonstration. Hell, he didn't mind volunteering. He needed the massage. Every muscle in his body was tighter than a woman's corset thanks to that kiss he gave Cassie.

"We'll start with the shoulders and back of the neck, and then work our way down the spine." She rubbed her palms together and the scent of mint oil filled the air as it warmed.

The sun heated his back and as soon as she touched his shoulders he closed his eyes. She had a great tech-

nique and strong hands as she kneaded the bunched
up muscles.

"My, oh, my, you are so tense." Mary Jane dug her
thumb into a particularly nasty knot. "Cassie, you really need to give this poor man more massages."

"Gee, just what I was thinking," Cassie said, her
caustic tone making the other women laugh.

Dalton opened one eye and angled his face toward
her. She stood with her hands folded across her chest,
an aggravated look on her face. She hadn't spoken to
him for the past hour, which suited him just fine. She
was too damn nosy. Thought she knew how to get
inside his head.

Instead of closing his eyes again, he let his gaze rest
on her legs. Super toned, very sexy.

"Try to relax, Dalton." Mary Jane dug into him
again and this time he winced. "You're all knotted up.
See this muscle here," she said to the others, and Simone and Kathy moved closer. Not Cassie, though.
She didn't budge.

"It's one of the largest and can get really tight.
Sometimes you'll need to use your elbow like this."

Dalton nearly leaped off the table. He rolled over to
his side. "Hey, you trying to cripple me?"

"It's important to get you to relax." She turned to
the women. "The more relaxed your partner is, of
course the better he'll be able to perform."

Surely Dalton hadn't heard correctly. He looked at
Cassie. Her hand was partially hiding her mouth, but
he caught the smile.

He turned a peevish look on Mary Jane. "I can perform just fine without you bruising me."

"Oh, I'm not trying to do that," she said with a somber shake of her head. "That kind of foreplay doesn't come up until Wednesday's session."

"You're kidding, right?"

She smiled. "Hey, you men don't have to hang back. Step up closer where you can see what I'm doing. Women have the same muscle groups, you know."

Even Tom didn't look anxious to come forward, and Dalton knew precisely why. The view of Mary Jane's round bare cheeks from his current vantage point was hard to give up.

Cassie had an even better backside, he thought lazily. Of course he hadn't seen it. Not au naturel like Mary Jane's, but even in jeans it looked damn near perfect.

Shit, he had to get his thoughts off that track. Last night, sharing the same bed had been much harder than he'd thought it would be. Even a foot away and his back to her, her musky feminine scent and heat had gotten to him.

A couple of times she'd touched his leg and he'd nearly pulled her into his arms and slid his hand up her nightshirt. It had driven him crazy wondering what she had on underneath the baggy pink shirt. She would've had something on, panties maybe. Or maybe she'd really chickened out and wore shorts. He'd been so damned tempted to find out he'd ached half the night.

Thinking about Cassie and last night was starting to make him hard. God help him if Mary Jane asked him to flip over right now.

The men finally started shifting closer, and Dalton started to relax again under Mary Jane's practiced hands. He had to admit, she was really good. When she'd claimed to be a licensed masseuse he hadn't believed it. Nevertheless, he was anxious to have Cassie's hands on him.

Dammit. He had to stop thinking like that. Better he remember the unrealistic way she viewed relationships and marriage. Of course he wasn't thinking of her in those terms. He just wanted to get naked with her.

Mary Jane worked the muscles on either side of his spine, down to his waist, while explaining the different muscle groups to the group. Frankly, he doubted anyone cared about the correct anatomical names. He sure didn't, but that didn't stop her.

Mary Jane gave his back a pat and then stood back. "Cassie, come over here, please."

"I can see just fine from here," Cassie replied tartly.

Mary Jane chuckled. "This is a hands-on exercise."

"And you're doing a wonderful job."

Simone and Zelda laughed. Kathy leaned toward Cassie and whispered something that made her blasé expression waver.

"It's too damn hot to be out here," Grant said from the sidelines. "Why we couldn't do this in the house is beyond me."

Tom and Zelda murmured agreement.

Mary Jane waved off their objections. "It's so much better out here because—where are you going?"

"Inside to get something to drink." Grant had already crossed the deck and headed toward the path to the house.

"Wait. Grant, stop." Mary Jane's voice rose in panic.

Grant turned around and drew his head back in surprise. Everyone else stared just at her. Oddly, she really seemed to be upset about Grant returning to the house. Dalton glanced at Cassie. Her eyebrows furrowed in thought, she frowned curiously at Mary Jane. He'd bet anything Cassie was thinking the same thing he was. *Bask is up to something back at the house.*

The other woman seemed to gather her composure and smiled, and said, "The gazebo is fully stocked with everything from scotch to soft drinks."

Grant frowned. "I'd really like some of Tasha's mint iced tea."

"Sorry, you can't go in the kitchen right now." Totally calm again, Mary Jane gave him a sympathetic smile. "Tasha is washing the kitchen floor while we're out here. That's part of the reason we utilize this area for the massages. So she can do some light housekeeping while we're all out of her hair."

And what was Bask doing while they were occupied? Dalton's gaze strayed toward the house. All he could see was the second floor over the trees and shrubs.

"I'd like something to drink, too," he said and rolled off the table.

Mary Jane made a not-so-charming sound of annoyance. "But we aren't done."

"I am." He grabbed a towel and tried rubbing off some of the oil from his back and legs.

"Y'all are being most uncooperative," Mary Jane said, putting her hands on her hips. "We really need to stay in the spirit of reconnecting. I suggest we take a break, have something to drink from the gazebo bar, and then—Dalton, wait, the gazebo is that way."

"Don't worry. I won't mess up Tasha's floor."

"But Dalton—"

He ignored her and skirted the pool to get to the path. He didn't make it. He heard Mary Jane's shriek of laugher just as she pushed him into the water.

He sank to the bottom and felt a nearby splash. Good thing it was the deep end of the pool. Good thing he knew how to swim. He opened his eyes on the way back up and saw that Mary Jane had followed him in. The friggin' nutcase.

He bobbed his head above the surface in time to hear her say, "Come on in, everyone, the water is nice and warm."

Simone quickly took up the suggestion, landing in the pool close to Dalton, sans bikini top. Harvey jumped in right behind her.

Dalton swam to the edge of the pool and looked around for Cassie. She was nowhere in sight.

His gaze went toward the path to the house and he caught a fleeting glimpse of her as she disappeared into the foliage.

He smiled. Good girl.

CASSIE HEARD noise coming from the kitchen—Tasha clanging pots and humming, and what sounded like a low male voice. Hoping it was Bask and not a radio, Cassie hurried upstairs, although what she expected to find she had no idea. All she knew was that Mary Jane seemed to be trying her best to keep everyone away from the house.

The second floor was as quiet as a church. Doors were closed, including the one to hers and Dalton's room. She peeked inside, trying to figure out if anything had been disturbed. Damn, she wished she'd left the bed unmade. If Tasha had been in tidying up, it was harder to tell.

One thing that seemed different was the door to the closet. It was open, but Cassie could swear she'd closed it. She glanced inside the closet. Someone had messed with her suitcase, she was fairly certain. Not that they'd find anything. She'd been careful about what she'd packed, but the idea was still unnerving.

After poking around for a few minutes, she braved her way to Bask's office on the third floor. Risky, because there was no reason for her to be up there, but this was her chance to finally do her own investigating and she wasn't about to forgo the opportunity.

She took a deep breath and rehearsed a quick excuse in her head in case she got caught.

Good thing.

Just as she reached for the doorknob, Bask opened the door. She jerked back and put a hand to her throat. "You startled me."

He seemed pretty startled himself, but he just smiled. "I thought everyone was outside."

"I was. They are." She took a deep breath. "I need to talk to you."

"But you don't want to miss massage class." He started to pull the door closed behind him.

"Being here is pointless. I was wrong to insist Dalton and I come here. Our marriage is over."

"Now, now, don't be so hasty."

She sniffed. "Can I come in?"

He hesitated. "Are you sure you don't want to finish massage class and meet later?"

She nodded, even more curious now as to why he didn't want her in his office. "I'd rather talk to you."

"Of course. Give me just a moment to straighten up." He gave her one of his "charming" smiles and then disappeared, closing the door behind him.

Cassie muttered a curse. She wasn't going to get anywhere now that he knew she was in the house. Except maybe open the door for Bask to approach her. She sighed. That hadn't been her objective. Unfortunately, that was her only hope of making any headway with him.

A couple of minutes later he opened the door again, his smarmy smile in place as he stepped aside to let her pass him. "Please, come in."

He gestured her to a chair facing his desk, and fortunately not the couch against the opposite wall. He waited for her to sit before he took his own seat behind the desk.

She sighed. "I wish Dalton was as gentlemanly and

courteous as you. With all his family's money you'd think he would have learned some manners.''

"Now, Cassie, I'm sure Dalton has many other good qualities."

"Name them."

Bask laughed. "You married him. Something attracted you."

"It wasn't the money," she said quickly. "I've never been a pauper myself."

"Of course not." He waved a dismissive hand. "If it were just about money you wouldn't be here." He paused, pursing his lips. "Although I trust you won't be left destitute should the marriage not remain intact."

"I'm not foolish, Mr. Blankenship. I'll be well provided for." And then she quickly added, "But it really isn't about the money."

"Please call me Robert." His smile gentled. "I understand. You want Dalton to pay attention to you." His gaze wandered briefly to her chest. "You're a beautiful woman, Cassie. You deserve his attention."

Her blush was genuine. At least she could report to Jennifer that Bask had a wandering eye. He gave her the creeps. She wanted to get up and run back to the pool but she forced a smile and a sigh. "You really need to give him lessons in charm."

"You flatter me—"

Behind him, the fax machine started. He snapped his gaze around to the paper sliding out. When he faced her again, he seemed nervous. "Cassie, why don't you give Dalton a chance." He got up and came around the desk. "At least complete the week," he added distractedly.

"I suppose I could…"

He extended a hand, and when she took it, he pulled her to her feet. "Please excuse me. I have some urgent business to attend to. We'll talk again later, all right?"

"Of course." She gave him a girlie smile. "Robert."

He squeezed her hand and walked her to the door. "Go enjoy the massage class."

After the door closed, she heard the lock click.

Damn!

"I HOPE Y'ALL do better with your one-on-one sessions," Mary Jane said, while wringing out her wet hair. "Most of our guests love to learn the art of massage."

After Grant and Tom joined the party, their romp in the pool had lasted nearly forty minutes, mostly thanks to Dalton. He kept the playful water fights going long after Mary Jane had wanted to call it quits. Zelda and Kathy never did join them in the water, which turned out for the best because Mary Jane still hadn't appeared to notice that Cassie was missing.

Dalton kept his eye out for her return and as soon as he thought he saw her hovering behind a tree, he grabbed a towel.

"Hey, M.J., let me help you dry your back."

She turned to look at him with wide startled eyes, and then a tiny smile played at the corners of her mouth. "Sure."

She started to turn around to give him her back, but

he quickly threw the towel around her to keep her prisoner, facing him, to keep her from spying Cassie. He rubbed her back with the towel, and then drew it over her buttocks. Mary Jane pressed her breasts against him, and over her shoulder he watched Cassie slip back into the group.

Zelda gave him a nasty look of disapproval. Simone's stare was murderous. She still hadn't put her top back on and her nipples stuck out to Alaska. He looked away and focused on Cassie as he stepped away from Mary Jane.

"There you go. All nice and dry."

At his abrupt withdrawal, she pursed her lips in a pout. "I think you might have missed a couple of spots."

"Sorry." He handed her the towel and went to sit beside Cassie.

Mary Jane's gaze followed him and she frowned suddenly, probably realizing she hadn't seen Cassie for over half an hour.

He put his arm around Cassie's shoulders and kissed the side of her neck. She started to pull away until he whispered, "Find anything?"

She stilled and then snuggled against him. "I think Bask may have gone through our room."

"Just ours?"

"I don't know." She shifted positions and made a face at something near the pool. "I wish Simone would put her damn top on."

"Why?"

"You have to ask?"

He shrugged. "The more distractions the better.

Even ol' Tom there is having trouble keeping his eyes strictly on his wife.''

"Oh, so maybe I should take my shirt off, too. Give them all something new to look at while you go nose around.''

"Sure. Not a bad idea.''

She reached for the hem of her T-shirt but he stopped her. "Nah, you don't have to do that.''

"I don't mind.''

He held on to her hand. "Don't do it, Cassie.''

"Why not?''

"I don't want you to.''

"Ah, gee, you should have told me right off the bat. That would have been reason enough.'' She rolled her eyes skyward, shook free of him and continued to lift her shirt high enough that he caught a glimpse of pink lace before he grabbed her hand again, this time a little too harshly.

"What's the matter with you?'' She tried to twist out of his grasp. "I'm only trying to help.''

What the hell was the matter with him? Why should he care if she took off her shirt, her bra or any other garment she wanted to? She wasn't his wife. She wasn't even his girlfriend. And yet the thought of any of the pecker-head men at this low-rent Shangri La taking a look at Cassie's bare breasts made him see red. Hell, he was nuts. He'd never been jealous a day in his life. Not even with Linda, when he'd had good reason to be. What he needed was to get a damn grip.

He let her go and rubbed the back of his neck. This was not good. Not good at all.

She studied him for a minute. "Okay, if it bothers you that much, I won't." She tugged her shirt back down, which solved the obvious problem. It didn't do squat to relieve what was going on inside his head. The only thing he could think to do was get them back on track. He put his arm around her shoulders again and drew her close. "About Bask. What makes you think he'd been in our room?"

"My suitcase isn't the way I left it," she said and then shocked him by kissing the side of his jaw.

He jerked back to look at her and she kissed him on the mouth. Not hard but determined enough to get his ticker going in full gear.

"Relax," she whispered, her lips curving into a coy smile. "I don't want our little tête-à-tête to look suspicious."

"Right." Right, his ass. What was she up to? Shit, was he that obvious about being—he couldn't even say the word.

"Of course Tasha may have been straightening the room. But my suitcase was in the closet. There'd be no reason for her to go in there."

"Unless she's nosy."

"Maybe..." She lightly bit his earlobe, and then laved it with her tongue.

"Cassie, what are doing?"

"I told you." She ran the tip of her tongue around his ear which had a direct connection to his cock, it seemed, as his pants got tighter by the second.

"All you're doing is calling attention to us."

"Hmm?"

He closed his eyes, willing his hard-on away. She had to know how turned on he was getting. What the hell was she doing? Was this payback?

"Hey, you two," Mary Jane called in an impatient voice. "We're ready to resume here."

"Ooh, *resume,* big word for her," Cassie whispered as she ignored Mary Jane and trailed her lips along his jaw to his mouth.

She tilted her head and teased his lips open with her tongue. She took her time, sweeping the inside of his mouth, sucking his lower lip and biting it lightly.

"Excuse me." Mary Jane stood a foot away, waited for them to break it up and glared at Cassie. "You'll have plenty of time for that later."

Cassie arched her brow. "Sorry, I didn't hear you." She stood and extended her hand to Dalton. "Come on, honey, we're getting to the good part."

She lifted her chin as she led him back toward the pool, leaving Mary Jane to stare after them with a murderous glint in her eyes.

"I get it," Dalton said when they were out of earshot. "You're jealous."

"Oh, please." She released his hand.

"You are. You're jealous because of the massage and the way she—"

Cassie stopped and faced him, her hand up. "Wait a minute. In order for me to be jealous wouldn't that mean I'd have to at least like you?" She gave him a smug smile. "Case closed."

He grinned. "Denial isn't just a river in Egypt."

"Oh, how clever. I'm going to tell you one more

time. That was an act so that we could talk privately. Besides, I promised Robert I'd come back to class and at least try to be civil.''

Dalton grunted, and then her words registered. "You spoke to him?''

"Yep.''

"Just now?''

She nodded. "So it doesn't matter if Mary Jane knows I left the group.''

"Did he catch you snooping?'' he asked and she shook her head. "What did he say?''

"Nothing important, unfortunately. Besides, we can't talk right now.'' Cassie started to head toward the others again. He caught hold of her hand and drew her back to him.

"Come on, sweetheart, how about another kiss?'' he said loudly, and then whispered, "What the hell happened?''

"Later.''

He kissed her hard, trying to let her know she couldn't brush him off so easily. If she had information, he wanted it.

She gave him a smile that made him uneasy as she snuggled closer, placing her hands on his chest. One hard shove and he stumbled backward. A second later he was back in the pool.

9

"OKAY, NOW WE BREAK into couples," Mary Jane said, "and practice what we've learned about massage and touching."

Cassie inclined her head toward Dalton and muttered, "If she says *we* one more time I may have to hurt her."

He didn't respond. He was probably still ticked off over falling into the pool an hour ago. Why should she care? He'd asked for it. As if he hadn't been trying to goad her...

"Explain what you mean by breaking into couples." Harvey grinned. "Does it have to be with your wife?" Zelda elbowed him and he grunted with the jab. "I was only joking, honey bunny."

"I don't know why she puts up with him," Cassie whispered to Dalton, already forgetting that he wasn't speaking to her.

"Zelda's the one with the money. He doesn't have a cent."

"How do you know?"

"Simone told me."

"When did you talk to her?"

"When you disappeared this morning during our

session." *Like a sulky child,* she thought, but wisely didn't verbalize.

"Find out anything else?"

"Just chit-chat girl stuff. Nothing useful."

Mary Jane kept giving them dirty looks as she explained to the group the importance of reconnecting through what she called courtship-touching. If they kept up their little sidebar, she'd probably ask if they had anything they'd like to share with the class.

"One more thing." Dalton shifted so that their shoulders touched, and to Cassie's utter amazement, she had a little tingling reaction. "Did you have anything in your suitcase or purse that would be incriminating?"

"Of course not." That chafed. She wasn't a rookie. Well, not really. "Did you?"

"Seriously, you don't have any ID or anything that would compromise us."

"Seriously, *no.*" Her reply came out more harshly than she intended.

His expression softened. "Look, I'm sorry if I hurt your feelings. I just don't want any surprises."

His lack of confidence did hurt. She only regretted that he'd apparently seen it in her face. She focused on Mary Jane and tried not to think about the heavy feeling in her chest.

It didn't work. She couldn't let go of the hurt. Dalton had really disappointed her, and worse, to a degree more than she understood. Would he have asked one of his colleagues from the bureau that same question? Of course not. He'd have assumed that he or she knew better than to pack anything that would blow their cover.

"Hey." He nudged her shoulder with his. "By the way, good work going to the house and checking on our boy."

The unexpected praise eased some of the ache. But she wasn't so sure he hadn't said that to placate her.

He leaned his head closer again. "How can you tell that a blonde used the computer last?"

She turned to look at him in amazement. And she'd thought he wanted to soothe her. What a jackass.

"Give up? There's whiteout on the screen."

Cassie shook her head in disgust and looked straight ahead into Mary Jane's annoyed gaze. She'd stopped talking and everyone turned around to look at Cassie and Dalton.

"Did you have a question about erogenous zones?" she asked with a teacher's sternness.

They were talking about erogenous zones? Wow, Cassie really hadn't been paying attention.

Neither had Dalton from the expression on his face. But he quickly masked his surprise and gave a casual shrug. "No, just telling blonde jokes. Want to hear them?"

Mary Jane was not pleased and she had no qualms showing it.

"Why don't you come up here and show us what you know?"

"About?"

"Erogenous zones."

"Show?" He laughed. "You mean tell?"

"I've already done the telling part. But you seem to be such an expert you haven't needed to pay attention." She motioned for him to approach. "Maybe we can all benefit from your expertise."

This was definitely yet another side to Mary Jane. A hard edge to her even changed her looks somewhat. She wasn't the perky cheerleader type everyone despised in high school, but more the firm authoritarian.

Dalton didn't say a word. Whether because he was still assessing the situation, or because she'd caught him off guard, Cassie didn't know.

"This is stupid," Cassie said, drawing the woman's attention away from Dalton. "All this seems like is an excuse for an orgy."

Simone chuckled. "Don't knock it until you've tried it, honey."

Dalton smiled, and glancing over at Cassie, said loud enough for everyone to hear, "Coming here was your idea if you recall."

"Yes, and I was wrong. We're leaving."

"Wait." Mary Jane rushed over before Cassie could even turn around. "I apologize if I was rude."

"It doesn't matter. This just isn't our thing. Come on, Dalton." She made as if she was leaving.

He caught her hand and pulled her back. "But, darlin', we didn't get to the naked part yet."

"You're a pig."

His mouth curved in a cocky smile. "One of the many things you like about me."

"We're wasting our time." Cassie shook her head

and tried to look sad, or at least resigned. "This marriage is over."

"Wait. But this is only the second day," Mary Jane said, all sugary sweet again. "I can't lose clients on the second day. Mr. Blankenship would fire me. You wouldn't want me to get fired, would you?"

"Cassie, we're already here." Dalton tugged at her hand and she stumbled toward him. "I promise I'll be more serious about this."

"I don't know," she said slowly.

He slid his arms around her waist and nuzzled her neck.

"Come on, honey, I don't want our marriage to be over. I'll do anything you want."

"Well." She instinctively stretched her neck to the side to give him better access. "Okay. We'll try one more day."

"That's my baby," he murmured against her skin.

And God help her, she could barely remember this was just a role. Dammit, she didn't know the exact moment when it happened, but she wanted him. More than she'd ever wanted a man. All the teasing and touching and kissing had finally gotten to her and the craving for his touch was like an itch she had to scratch.

She'd never been particularly bold or assertive when it came to sex, but this was the perfect opportunity. After all, Dalton *was* supposed to be her husband.

Hell, she was going for it.

DALTON CLOSED their bedroom door behind him. He could still hear Mary Jane in the hall, cheering on the other couples as she escorted them to their rooms. He shook his head. As if they all didn't know what to do behind closed doors.

He looked at Cassie. She'd gone straight for the carafe of water sitting on the mini-refrigerator and poured some into a glass.

She took a big gulp, and then asked, "You want one?"

"Sure." He locked the door against Mary Jane's orders.

Cassie smirked. "She'll only bang on it."

"She can bang away." He crossed the room and accepted the glass of ice-cold water. "Thanks."

"Now what?"

"We get naked."

Cassie opened her mouth to make some snide remark, judging from the look on her face, but he put a finger to her lips and mouthed...*careful*.

She jerked away. "Okay." And then shocked the hell out of him by pulling off her T-shirt. Her pink lace bra was cut low and the mounds of tempting flesh facing him had him gritting his teeth.

"What are you doing?" His voice was so hoarse it was barely recognizable.

"Exactly what you suggested." She wedged her hands in the elastic waistband of her shorts and shoved them down her legs, and then stooped to snatch them from around her ankles. In that position, her breasts nearly fell out of the small lacy cups.

She straightened and cast the shorts aside. Her pant-

ies matched the bra. Pink lace. Very tiny. Her waist
was much smaller than the jeans let on. She was stunning. And he was seconds away from cardiac arrest.

He took a deep steadying breath. "Okay, hold on."

"Yes?"

"Don't give me that innocent look."

She made a face and quietly shushed him. She
crooked her finger for him to come closer.

No way. He took a step back.

She whispered, "I thought you had something to
say."

He tried keeping his eyes face level. Not in this
lifetime. His gaze had a will of its own, running the
length of her body, lingering on her perfect thighs. She
worked out, that was certain, but not so much that she
was too muscled.

And he noticed she really was a true blonde.

She moved toward him and he knew he should dis-
courage any contact, but he wasn't sure he was capable. As it was, he didn't have to worry. She stopped
half a foot away and looked expectantly at him.

He told himself not to look at her breasts. He didn't
listen. His gaze dove down her tempting cleavage. Beneath the thin silk, her nipples pearled and strained
against the fabric.

What would she do if he reached for the clasp, freed
her breasts, took the tips in his mouth?

Shit, this wasn't good. This was trouble. "Would
you explain why you—" He cleared his throat, remembered to keep his voice low. "Why you—" He
waved a hand, gesturing to her seminudity.

She lifted her shoulder in a casual shrug calling attention to her breasts. "It's part of our exercise."

"And you're willing to go along with Mary Jane's instructions?"

"To some degree. If she pays us a visit we'd better be prepared."

"That's why I locked the door."

She smiled. "Wouldn't it be simpler to get in bed and pretend we're...you know, getting cozy?"

The fit of his jeans was getting more uncomfortable by the second. "What are you up to?"

"Me?" Her eyes widened. "What?"

"You were the one so concerned about how, shall we say, *realistic* our performances had to be." Was he really trying to talk her out of this?

"Yes? And?"

"So what the hell are you doing?"

She frowned. "Keep it down." She got closer and whispered, "I'm sure you've seen a woman in her underwear before."

"No, this is my first time," he joked, trying to take his mind off his erection.

"Go ahead, be sarcastic and flip. I'm used to your defensiveness."

"My what?" He was about to tell her what a kook she was, but she raised a hand for silence and let out a loud, sensual groan.

She closed her eyes. "Ooh, baby, that feels so good." And then she opened them and asked in a much quieter, less throatier voice, "What were you going to say?"

He stared at her, totally speechless.

She shrugged a shoulder and whispered, "Just in case anyone's listening."

He continued to stare, for the life of him, unable to remember what he'd been about to say.

"You know, the carafe has been refilled," she whispered apparently oblivious to his amazement. "So it isn't as if anyone tried to hide the fact they were in the room. Of course that would be pretty smart. Are we going to stand here for the next two hours, or can we...get comfortable?"

Obviously a rhetorical question because she immediately headed for the bed. His gaze riveted to the slight sway of her hips. No thong, but her panties were so skimpy it showed off plenty of curvy flesh. How the hell did she expect him to have a normal conversation with her?

Oh, yeah. He recalled now what he'd been saying. "What are you *doing?*"

She put a frantic finger to her lips and motioned him closer as she sat on the edge of the bed and reached over to turn on the radio, he figured to muffle their whispers.

He had no choice but to comply if they wanted to have a decent conversation over the oldies station she found. As if anything they discussed would make any sense. His jeans had grown uncomfortably tight and she'd have to be blind not to notice.

Just as he gingerly sat about a foot away from her, she let out another one of her loud, sexy, throaty groans. "Oh, yes, honey, right there. Oh, baby, don't stop. Oh, yes, yes. Again."

She blinked at him, looking as if she'd simply informed him of the time of day.

Dalton realized he'd been holding his breath and let it out slowly. "You do that too well. It's damned scary."

She smiled. "Most women can."

"Right." A sobering thought. His gaze drifted downward, lingering on the way her nipples poked at the pink lace. Shit! This wasn't going to work. He got up, but she caught his hand and tugged him back down.

"Dalton..." She leaned forward and kissed his jaw. "Take off your shirt."

Bad idea. He pulled the polo over his head so fast he heard one of the buttons pop. "I already explained. I don't mix business with pleasure."

"I know." She kissed him briefly on the lips and put her hand on his chest.

"So what exactly are we doing?" he asked, beginning to care less and less.

"This is business." She kissed him again, too briefly and then leaned back and said, "Just a minute."

This time her moaning was even more sensual, more heart-stopping. She even threw in a head toss as she cried out, "I can't take it. Stop. No, don't. Oh, oh, baby, oh, you don't know what you're doing to me." She delivered three throaty pants followed by a smile and a shrug.

She cocked her head to the side and whispered, "It wouldn't hurt if you made some noise, too."

He squinted at her. "Why the sudden change in attitude?"

She pressed her palm against his chest and made little circles until his nipple responded. "I don't know. I figure there might as well be perks with the job. It's not like it would hurt anything. Make our roles more believable if nothing else."

"Ah." *Brilliant comeback, Styles.* "What about the distraction thing?" Another sultry look like the one she just gave him, and he wouldn't give a shit about anything.

"We're supposed to be distracted right now. By each other." She let the side of her hand trail down the shallow valley between his nipples toward the waistband of his shorts. "Besides, we're stuck in the room. There's not much else we can do."

God, he wanted to see her breasts. Without the bra. He wanted to close his mouth around her nipples, suck her like a lollipop. "Cassie…" His voice came out ragged and broken. "I hope you know what you're doing."

She pushed up against him, her breasts rubbing his chest and her tongue touching his lips. He opened his mouth and drew her tongue inside and ran his hands down the soft skin over her rib cage, the indention of her waist, the curve of her hip.

He moaned when she cupped his erection and stroked his cock through his shorts. He toyed with the leg elastic of her panties, slipping a finger inside until it met soft springy hair. She stiffened slightly as he stroked her gently.

"Cassie, honey, take off your bra."

She drew back without dislodging his hand and regarded him through glazed eyes. Her lips were moist and shiny, her flushed cheeks making her eyes incredibly blue. "What if this doesn't work? It'll affect our attitude toward each other."

"Huh?" The bra looked as if it had a front clasp, but everything was so small these days you couldn't always tell.

"Are you listening to me?"

"What?"

"Dalton."

He looked into her eyes and saw doubt. Big time. He continued his soft strokes, petting her like a tamed kitten. "What's wrong?"

"I know I started this…" She nibbled her lower lip and swiped at her tangled hair.

He brushed it away from her cheek with his free hand. "But you think it's a mistake," he finished for her.

"No." She pressed her lips together. "I have no idea why I—" She groaned. "I don't even like you. I don't."

"Thanks."

She looked away, her face filling with color. "I don't know what's wrong with me. I'm not myself."

"This is an odd situation. We've been thrown together among a group of kooks, who are all strangers. That sort of undermines the fact that we were strangers until five days ago. Now we're sort of co-conspirators." He shrugged, amazed that he could have this conversation while his fingers were between her legs and his mind was spinning. "We have only each other to speak freely, to trust, to understand what's going on. Of course you might have feelings develop."

She frowned. "You don't."

"What?"

"Have any feelings."

He exhaled slowly. "Look, agents who go under-cover are sometimes pulled off their assignment because they get too close to the people they're supposed to be investigating. They get attached, disarmed by the perp's human frailties. It's natural."

"Of course." She looked down, and murmured, "So all this will pass after the case."

"Sure."

"So we just have to worry about looking like a real married couple."

He frowned, not sure what she was getting at. It sounded a lot like rationalization. He nudged her chin up until their eyes met. "I'm only worried about the fastest way to get that bra off you. And not so I can do your laundry."

That startled a laugh out of her.

"You have no idea what kind of wicked things I want to do to you." To illustrate, he moved his finger an inch, to the cleft itself, already moist. He dipped inside, just for a second, although once he'd felt that wet velvet, it was all he could do not to rip their clothes off and take her.

She openly shivered, and her lips parted with a moan. He kissed them lightly, briefly, reminding himself this could be a big mistake. He should stop. He couldn't.

"What about not mixing business with pleasure?"

"I figure this is both." He found the clasp with his left hand and undid it, then pushed the lacy cups aside.

She gasped but didn't resist when he palmed her breast. She was soft yet firm, her nipple so responsive, he thought he might come before he got his friggin' pants off.

When she ran her hand over his erection, he knew he was in deep trouble. He lowered his mouth to her nipple and suckled it until she whimpered.

Still kissing her, he used his weight to lay her back, head on pillow, body open and ready for his next move. She tried to reach for his fly but he wouldn't let her touch him. Not yet. Not until he'd had his fill of her.

If that were even possible.

The sudden thought rattled him.

This was a perk, mutual chemistry that would make their roles all the more believable. That's all. No analysis necessary. She tasted so damn good....

A knock at the door made them both start.

"How are you two doing?" Incredibly, it was Mary Jane.

Cassie stiffened. "Can you believe her?"

"Don't answer." He sucked in her other nipple and slid his finger up until he found her clitoris.

Another knock. "Hey, you two had better not have fallen asleep."

"We have to answer or she won't go away."

Dalton didn't care. He'd just tune her out. What he was doing was much more important. He circled her nub, and Cassie squirmed beneath him.

"Cassie? Dalton? You don't have much more time."

Cassie opened her mouth as a slow smile curved her lips. She closed her eyes as he continued to stroke her, then, put a hand to her throat and let out a loud sexy moan. For real. "Oh, and, deeper, come on, deeper. Oh, oh…" She moaned again, and he let himself relax into her, circling her flesh insistently.

She whimpered, moaned, panted. "Don't stop. Please, again, deeper this time. Oh, baby…" Something shifted. Her body tensed around him, and when he looked up, he saw her face and neck flush, her eyes closed. The tone of her moaning changed, deepened, and he smiled. Almost there.

He took her nipple gently between his teeth, and flicked his tongue at the same rapid tempo as his finger. He wanted her to come, to hear the real sounds of Cassie as she climaxed. He might just join her without even touching himself.

Her breathing quickened, her hands gripped the bedspread, and her muscles grew as taut as bowstrings. "Dalton, oh God. What are you— Please, right there. Just a little… Oh, God."

He picked up the pace with his hand, and let up on her nipple so he could see her face. A second later, her body arched off the bed in a spasm. She cried out, inarticulate and so, so sweet. He was so turned on by her face, her moans, he felt like he was going to explode. But he held off. This was for Cassie.

Her hand went to his wrist, and he stopped rubbing her. But she didn't stop shaking. Trembling. She opened her eyes and gave him a look of pure, unadulterated satisfaction.

He grinned, and that's when her rosy flush turned crimson.

Maybe it had been a mistake. Maybe it hadn't been good for the case. But dammit, he didn't care. Now that he'd seen her like this, he was hooked. He'd make her come again. And again. Or die trying.

10

CASSIE SAT directly across from Dalton at dinner, wondering if she had totally lost her mind. The guy irritated her. He told blonde jokes, for goodness sakes. And now, she'd blown everything all to hell and back by having an orgasm!

It was her own damn fault, too. She'd been so sure of herself. So cocky. Taking off her blouse like that. Making sexy noises. It served her right.

Her face heated again as she remembered the feel of him, the way he'd known exactly how to touch her. How could she go back to the room tonight? And how on earth could they go back to the way they were before….

She'd totally given up so much as glancing at him. Twice now she'd embarrassed herself by stuttering over a question after having lost track of the dinner conversation.

After another embarrassed glance, she pulled herself together. It wasn't that big a deal, for heaven's sake. Why shouldn't she have something with Dalton that was strictly physical? She wasn't looking for a relationship, and certainly neither was he, so what was the harm?

"Cassie?"

She looked blankly at him.

"Would you like more potatoes?" he asked, signaling with his eyes.

She jerked when she realized Tasha stood beside her with the bowl of mashed potatoes in one hand and a serving spoon in the other. "Uh, no thanks," she muttered, careful to avoid the others' curious gazes.

Mary Jane laughed. "Don't be embarrassed. Tasha is used to this kind of disorientation after the touching exercises. Amazing how it works, isn't it? You and Dalton can barely keep your eyes off each other."

Cassie forced herself to smile, the blush coming naturally. That was so not true. She'd purposely avoided him, hadn't she? She darted a look his way and saw that he seemed a little uncomfortable, too. Had he been watching her as Mary Jane suggested?

"Oh, it's just as sweet and touching as could be." Simone couldn't possibly look any more bored as she sipped her wine. As usual her food had barely been touched.

"Why don't you shut up?" Kathy startled everyone with her little outburst. She was usually so quiet, but her face was flushed and her blue eyes angry. "I don't even know why you're here, Simone, but you are, and making fun of the rest of us doesn't help anyone."

Simone's brows rose in amusement. "This afternoon was obviously good for you. It's nice not to see you being such a timid little mouse."

"Simone!" Mary Jane looked angrier than Cassie had ever seen her.

Tom glared at the redhead, his jaw tensed. "You're lucky you're a lady, or I'd have flattened you. But say something like that to my wife again and I may forget I'm a gentleman."

Grant chuckled. "He called you a lady, Simone. I believe that's a first."

She smiled in that bored-looking way of hers, clearly unfazed by either man's comment. But then she stared somewhere past Cassie, her expression suddenly wary.

"Simone, may I have a word with you?" It was Bask. He'd come through the kitchen door, his voice calm and controlled, but instantly getting Simone's attention.

She got up from the table and quietly followed him out of the dining room into the hall.

Cassie met Dalton's pensive eyes. They'd all been led to believe Bask had left for the evening.

"Well," Mary Jane said brightly. "Are we almost ready for dessert? I believe homemade strawberry shortcake is on the menu tonight."

No one answered at first. Kathy stared down at her plate, her face still red. Grant seemed oblivious to the fact that his wife had been called to the principal's office while he polished off his roast beef.

"I say bring on dessert. I don't know how much longer I can stay awake." Dalton made a show of stifling a yawn.

Cassie murmured her agreement. What the heck was he up to? He wasn't tired, that much she knew. The keen look he'd given Bask meant the wheels were turning in Dalton's head. She hoped he didn't have some stupid notion of following Bask. That would be useless, anyway. He probably returned home to Marianne's house each night.

Mary Jane promptly rang the bell and Tasha ducked in to get the signal for dessert. Within seconds she brought the strawberry shortcake out on a glass platter. It looked delicious. Too bad no one seemed as if they had an appetite. Except maybe for Grant.

The thought of his and Simone's disintegrating relationship depressed Cassie. They had to have loved and respected each other once. What happened in a marriage that made two people so indifferent to each other? Is this what she had to look forward to if she ever got married? It was both sad and scary.

Dalton wolfed down his shortcake as soon as Tasha served it. He told a beaming Tasha how fabulous she was and that if he weren't already married she'd have to watch out. Apparently she understood enough of what he'd said that she hummed her way back into the kitchen with the empty dinner plates.

Cassie had to admit that despite her own indifference toward the man, any woman would be proud to have a husband like Dalton. He never failed to thank Tasha for their meals, helped her carry anything heavy and was always quick with a joke when tension mounted within the group.

That proved it. She *was* crazy. Dangerous thinking. Very dangerous. Downright stupid.

As soon as Dalton stood, so did she. It was early yet, not totally dark, and she had no idea what he had in mind. She hoped to get him to go for a walk in the garden while they discussed their next step. If they went directly to the bedroom, there wouldn't be any talking...

"Don't forget that we all need to get up an hour earlier tomorrow morning," Mary Jane said, raising her voice to be heard over the sound of chairs moving and people murmuring.

"Why?" Harvey grimaced.

"Oh, didn't I tell you?" She gave them that wide bright smile that got on Cassie's nerves. "Tomorrow we're going on a little excursion."

She hadn't mentioned any sort of outing before now. They all looked at each other and then expectantly at her.

"We're going on a nature walk to learn about the birds and the bees."

"DAMMIT, I wish I knew if Bask has left already." Dalton stood at their bedroom window, staring outside through the part in the drapes. "I can only see part of the driveway from here, but it doesn't matter since he could have left anytime in the last hour."

Cassie had just come out of the bathroom after changing into her nightshirt. The radio was on for interference, but he'd spoken too loudly. She moved closer and whispered, "I could go ask Mary Jane. Tell her I had a couple of questions for him."

"Or I could go to the kitchen for something..." Dalton let the drapes fall into place and turned around.

"...and see if his car is still—" His voice trailing off, he stared at her.

"What?" She had decided against wearing a bra or shorts under her nightshirt. But he wouldn't know the difference, would he? And for goodness sakes, he'd already...

He noisily cleared his throat and turned back to the window. "I think I'll go see if his car is still in the carport."

"Dalton..."

"Yeah?" He wouldn't turn around.

"What's wrong?"

"Nothing."

"Nothing, my foot," Cassie insisted, feeling dejected. He obviously already regretted this afternoon. He'd kept his distance from her and had done nothing but talk business ever since they got to the room. God, she wanted to sink into the floor. "You look disgusted with me, or something.

"Disgust is not what I'm feeling, trust me."

"Would you please look at me?"

Slowly he turned around.

"What's wrong?"

He shoved a hand through his hair, looking uneasy. "You haven't finished telling me about your conversation with Bask today."

She moved closer still so she could lower her voice. "There's really nothing more. He clearly didn't want me in his office. Our conversation was short. I said I wanted out of the marriage. He said I should keep trying. The subject of money was skirted, but he got a fax and pretty much chased me out of his office.''

"That's it?"

"I told you I didn't have anything really." It hurt that his tone was suddenly all business, as if this afternoon hadn't happened.

His gaze ran down her body, lingering on her thighs.

She crossed her arms in a protective gesture. "I wish you'd tell me what's wrong."

He muttered a curse, and all at once he grabbed her arms and pulled her to him before she could react. He kissed her hard and deep and, when she sagged against him, his hands traveled down her back and under the hem of her shirt.

When he discovered she wore thong panties, he groaned and cupped her cheeks, pulling her hard against him. He was already aroused, growing harder by the second and she had trouble catching her breath.

"Dalton," she finally was able to whisper. "Maybe we shouldn't—"

He kissed her silent, his large hands squeezing her as if he couldn't get enough of her. Tempted to pull off her nightshirt, she wound her hands around his neck instead.

To her disappointment, he retreated, but only, she quickly realized so that he could slide his hands up the front of her body. He reached her breasts and palmed them, his sharp intake of breath turning her on as much as his urgent touch.

Her nipples responded instantly and he pinched the hardening nubs lightly between his thumbs and fingers.

She worked her hands under his shirt, running her palms over the swell of his pectoral muscles, experiencing the hardening of his nipples.

"Cassie, honey, take your shirt off." He'd barely got out the words as he kissed and nibbled the corners of her mouth, her jaw, the soft skin behind her ear. "I want to see you."

She grew so wet she wanted to forget that she had second thoughts. And instead, lie beside him, feel the length of him slide deep inside of her.

"Dalton, I don't— Oh. God." She arched her head back when he kneaded her breasts in a maddeningly sensual way that made her want to push him backward onto the bed and have her way with him. Screw being an adult.

Except this was not only an important case, but her first, and she didn't want to let Jennifer down.

He lowered his head and through the nightshirt, he suckled one of her nipples. She strained against him, wishing the damn fabric were out of the way.

Damn, damn, damn.

"Dalton." She kissed his forehead, trying to take some of the sting out of what she was about to say. "We need to talk."

He moved his mouth to her other breast and she closed her eyes. His hands remained under her shirt, kneading and touching and chipping away at her resolve.

"Dalton, did you hear me?"

He drew back, and she let out a breath mixed with relief and disappointment, but then he lifted her nightshirt and stared at her breasts. He kissed the crown of one, and then the other before letting her shirt fall back in place.

"I heard you," he said, raising his glassy gaze to hers.

"Having second thoughts?"

"No. Maybe. I'm just trying to be a professional here."

With a lightning-quick move, he had her against him, his tongue in her mouth and she melted into him. He broke contact almost as quickly and she stumbled without his support. "You mean like that?" He grinned.

She hadn't uttered a single protest. She'd dived right in. Embarrassed, she crossed her arms over her chest and looked away.

"Don't worry about it, honey. We've both got some thinking to do." He touched her cheek. "Besides, I have to go out for a while."

"Where?"

"Check out a hunch."

"Are you going to clue me in?"

"Later. I promise."

She didn't believe him. "You're leaving because of me, aren't you?"

"No." He gave his head an adamant shake. "That's why I wanted to know if Bask had left. I wanted to leave to make a phone call, ask one of my buddies at the bureau to check something for me."

"Oh." She rubbed her arms. He looked earnest enough, but she still didn't like that he'd be gone. "I'll do some reading while you're gone. If Mary Jane asks for you I'll tell her we had a fight and you left to cool off.''

His expression fell briefly, probably remembering how he'd taken off after their morning session. ''Good plan. I shouldn't be long.''

His gaze fell to her bare legs and his chest heaved. Abruptly he turned to leave.

''Dalton, wait.'' She went to him and got close enough to feel his heat, the warmth of his breath. She wanted desperately to kiss him again, but she wouldn't. ''We've been talking too loudly. They've heard everything.''

Guilt flickered in his eyes. He cleared his throat. ''About the bugging...there isn't any. It started as a joke and then when I realized we had to get cozy every time we wanted to talk and—ah, shit. I lied.''

Cassie smiled. ''I know.''

DALTON HADN'T BROUGHT his cell phone. He'd wanted nothing on him or in the car that might give him away. He drove to the convenience store he'd used earlier in town, where he'd bought a calling card and then used their payphone. He didn't like that it faced the street but he'd made sure Bask had left the house some time ago, and at least there wasn't much traffic.

He punched his old partner's cell phone number and waited for his friend to pick up.

''Hello.''

''Frank, it's me.''

''Hey, you back in Chicago?''

"Nope, still in Texas."

"So why are you calling so damn late?"

Dalton shook his head. It was only nine-thirty, but anything after nine was late to Frank.

"I know, but this is business. I have a couple of names I want you to check out for me."

"You working undercover?"

Dalton hesitated. Once again he hadn't followed procedure and informed his boss of his actions. Frank was a good guy. He wouldn't say anything, but Dalton didn't want to put him in the middle.

"Sort of."

"You're not working on the Bask case anymore?"

"That's what this is about."

Frank paused. "But you didn't tell the brass you went undercover and now you want me to get your info for you."

"I didn't say that."

Frank chuckled. "If you're worried about my pension, you should have thought about it before you roped me into helping you with that armored car heist arrest."

Dalton winced. "They knew you had nothing to do with the surprise raid. I told them you thought I'd gotten clearance from the bureau."

"Bullshit, Styles. They knew you weren't smart enough to have put that raid together by yourself."

Dalton sighed. "Frank, you gotta quit trying to cover for me. You're too damned close to retirement to muck it up."

"That's what Marie says. She told me I can't go

out and play with you anymore.'' The older man laughed. ''Hey, Marie, hand me that paper and pencil.''

''Tell her I said hey.''

''Hell, no, I don't want her to know it's you.''

Dalton smiled. There was a lot of truth in that sentiment. He'd known Frank's wife for almost ten years. He liked her a lot and he knew she liked him, inviting him over for most holidays, but she didn't want him getting her husband in trouble anymore. Who could blame her?

''Okay, shoot.''

''Two names. One is Simone Harding, about five-seven, auburn hair, green eyes, and I'd guess mid-thirties. She has a slight French accent but either it's phony or she's lived in the States a long time. She could have aliases, but I don't know for sure.''

''Hold on. I don't know shorthand.''

Dalton looked around as he waited for Frank to tell him to continue. Simone was probably just who she seemed to be…a pathetic lush looking for attention. But Cassie was right, she and Grant had no reason to be at the encounter. And this was supposed to be their second time? If they were really married, he hadn't met a couple less interested in trying to make their relationship work. It just didn't make sense.

That wasn't the only oddity that triggered his interest. There was a connection between Mary Jane and Simone he couldn't identify, as if Mary Jane had something over the other woman.

''Hey, you fall asleep, or what?''

Dalton switched the receiver to his other ear. "I take it you're ready."

"Shoot."

Dalton smiled when he heard Marie in the background telling him to stop using that word. They'd been married thirty-two years and seemed genuinely happy. He envied them. "Next is Grant Harding, dark hair, brown eyes, close to six feet, pushing forty."

"Married to Simone?"

"So they say."

"Ah. I'll find out. He's not French I take it."

"Nope."

"Any idea where he might be from?"

"Come on, Frank, if I knew that I would've given you the information. I haven't gone that soft working this friggin' fluff case."

His friend grunted. "You got shafted. No question about it. Higgins shouldn't have stuck you with the Bask case. Political, that's all it is. I'm glad I'm getting out next year."

"So is Marie."

"Yeah, she says hi, by the way. She figured out it was you."

Dalton checked his watch. "Sorry I don't have more for you to go on, but cross what I gave you with our lineup of grifters. Maybe we'll get lucky."

"First thing in the morning. I'm surprised you don't sound too put out with this assignment."

His first thought was of Cassie, knowing she was the reason. "I'm just trying to wrap it up and get Higgins off my back."

"Ah, hell, boy, don't tell me you're starting to grow up." Frank's uproarious laughter annoyed the hell out of Dalton.

"Could be. Scary thought, huh? Anyway, buddy, thanks, but I gotta get back."

"Call me tomorrow afternoon and I should have something for you."

"Thanks. Now, go kiss Marie for me."

"Yeah, yeah." He severed the connection.

Dalton hung up and got in the Jag but he didn't start it right away. He rested his head back and thought about Cassie. How could he feel as if he'd known her for a lifetime when they'd met less than a week ago?

Maybe because she didn't play games like some women did. She was out there with her opinions and observations, and she was comfortable with her body in a way he found totally sexy.

He remembered their parting words and smiled. Okay, so they had both engaged in a little game playing. He wondered when she'd figured out their room wasn't bugged. She was smart and had good instincts. She probably realized it wouldn't have been cost or time effective for Bask to have had the rooms bugged. He learned all he needed to know about each couple through the group and private sessions.

Besides, Bask's typical M.O. meant that he never stayed in one place long. Generally less than a year, long enough to woo some unsuspecting woman and then take off with the goods. Two of the couples had been through this encounter week twice. Obviously he had his sights on one of the wives, assuming Simone wasn't involved with the scam. If so, that left Zelda.

Kathy was a poor target. It was obvious she wanted too much to please Tom. It was also obvious she loved the guy.

Cassie still remained a good candidate. The thought irked him. Just thinking of her alone with Bask made Dalton want to punch the guy in his pretty boy face.

He started the Jag, even angrier with himself for allowing that kind of emotion in. He couldn't afford to think of Cassie as anything but a partner. Like he'd think of Frank.

Yeah, right. He was in so much damn trouble, he better wrap up this case quickly. In the meantime, he'd sleep on the floor.

11
_____

"MORNIN'," CASSIE MUMBLED as she rolled onto her back and stretched her arms over her head.

Dalton smiled. She wasn't really awake yet. He'd turned off the alarm two minutes before it was supposed to ring, but she must have heard him moving around.

He pulled the sheet up to her shoulders just in case her nightshirt had ridden up during the night. Bad enough he'd let himself climb into bed beside her two hours ago, he didn't need to test his mettle any more.

Her eyes drifted open and then closed again, and she made a soft whimpering sound that put his mind on a totally different and dangerous track. He slid out of bed.

At the sudden movement, she opened her eyes again, and then raised herself on her elbows. "What time is it?"

"Seven. You still look tired. Didn't you sleep well?" He'd worn a pair of sweats to sleep in, and now he pulled on a T-shirt.

She blinked a couple of times and her sleepiness started to clear. So did her memory of last night, judg-

ing by the accusation entering her yes. "I waited up
for you until after midnight."

"Yeah, well, I had trouble finding a payphone that
worked."

Not only did she look at him with disbelief written
across her face, but also she looked disappointed.

"Okay, that's a lie." He rubbed the back of his
neck. "I drove around for a couple of hours."

She arched her brows and waited expectantly.

What? She wanted more of an explanation? Shit.
"I'm a coward, okay? I didn't trust myself to come
back here too soon."

"Why?"

It was his turn to stare in disbelief.

"Why do you think?"

"I asked first."

"So it's okay for you to have second thoughts but
not me?" He smiled to take the sting out of his words
when her expression fell. "Or do you just want to hear
how beautiful and tempting you are?"

She sank down, pulled the covers over her face, and
muttered a muffled, "I do not. I know what I look like
in the morning, and it ain't pretty."

"You are so wrong." He tugged at the sheets, but
she wouldn't let go. "You have to come out some
time."

"No, I don't. I'm playing hooky today. I'm going
to tell Mary Jane I'm sick and need to stay in bed, and
then I'm going to sleep for five blessed more hours."

"Right, as if you're not the least bit curious about
this birds and bees excursion."

She pulled down the sheets. "What do you think that's about?"

"I have no idea."

"Those people are nuts. It's probably just another way to get us away from the house."

Dalton smiled at the way her hair tangled only on one side and tended to stick up. She had a couple of black smudges under her eyes but they were only noticeable because her skin was so smooth and flawless. "Or a way to cause friction between the couples."

"I don't get it. How can anyone believe that what we've done could help get a marriage back on track? I mean, the open discussions are good, but even they aren't facilitated correctly." She shook her head. "These aren't stupid people. Most of them are educated and affluent enough to be savvy."

"Desperation."

"To hold on to the marriage?"

"They aren't thinking clearly, and it takes only one partner to be charmed by Bask into signing up."

"That's so sad."

Dalton went to the closet to get some clothes. She'd never been married. She didn't understand how vulnerable a committed, forever-do-us-part relationship made a person. How good sense flies out the window, and you think and do things you'd never have dreamed possible.

Nasty business. Somebody ought to write about *that* in *Bride's Magazine.* He poked through his suitcase, not anxious to resume a conversation about the subject of marriage. He sure wished he knew what today's activities were about since he'd only brought two pairs of shorts.

"Dalton, are you coming out sometime this decade?"

He couldn't help but smile at her impatient tone. One thing about Cassie, you didn't have to guess where she was coming from.

"Good grief. How long does it take you to pick out clothes?"

He came out of the closet laughing. "Yep, you have the wife role down pat. On second thought, you sound more like a husband."

"Don't be sexist."

"Never."

"Right." She finger-combed her hair, tugging out the tangles. "You didn't tell me about last night."

That was another interesting thing about Cassie. With the puzzling exception of her need for approval on the job, she wasn't just comfortable with her body, but with herself in general. She didn't have to look her best at all times. Practical. Simple. He liked that about her.

Linda had spent hours grooming herself, applying makeup, getting manicures and pedicures, the whole nine yards, and he'd always preferred the way she looked when she first woke up in the morning. But when he'd tell her that, she never believed him.

"I fessed up and admitted I drove around." He shrugged. "What else did you want to know?"

Disappointment clouded her face. "So you really didn't check on a hunch?"

"Oh, that." Dammit. He was losing it. His thoughts were too much about her and not the case. "Yeah. I called a buddy of mine, my former partner in fact, and he's running a background check on Simone and Grant."

She nodded, clearly not surprised. "I figured. There's an odd undercurrent between Simone and Mary Jane. And then Bask pulled Simone aside last night. Something ain't kosher there."

He grinned. "Spoken like a true, hard-boiled detective."

"Hey, hey, no teasing the rookie."

"Yeah, right, a rookie. As if." He chuckled.

She gave him a startled look and then glanced away. "So I take it you'll have to call your friend some time today for the results?"

"Wait a minute...you really *are* a rookie?"

Her eyes grudgingly met his. "This is sort of my first case."

That explained a lot. But now he was even more impressed with her calm and poise.

"Technically it isn't." She made a sound of frustration. "I said that wrong. Technically it is my first case for this agency, but I've been in the business for a couple of years. Before, I was more of an assistant. I did the grunt work for this guy. He kept promising me I'd go solo but he never made good, and I finally got another job."

"Well, it was his loss. You've got good instincts and you're composed under pressure. I'd never have guessed you haven't been in the field a while."

Cassie's smile stretched so wide, it had to have set a record. "You'd better not just be saying that."

"Why would I?" He shrugged. "But I gotta admit, I'm glad I didn't know this at the go."

Her expression crumbled. "Because you wouldn't have trusted me to help with the assignment."

"Probably not. But I would have been wrong, and it would've been *my* loss."

She smiled again. "Well, you're right. It's Chet's loss now, the idiot."

"Your old boss?"

She nodded and something in her expression told him he might even have been more than a boss. "He asked me to stay, started with the list of promises again, but I told him to shove it."

"Good for you." He wanted to ask about this Chet guy, but he wouldn't. None of his business. Just like his former marriage was none of hers. No sense opening a can of worms.

"I guess I'd better get my lazy butt up. Unless I can talk you into playing hooky with me." She gave him a sly smile that was belied by her pushing the sheets aside and swinging her legs to the floor.

He knew he should've stayed in the closet longer. In vain he tried to look away. When she stretched her arms over her head, the hem of her nightshirt riding up almost to her panties, he had to give himself a good mental shake.

"I have another confession to make," he said when she didn't seem in any hurry to get moving. "There is nothing I want to do more right now than to crawl back into bed and strip you naked.''

She blinked. ''Oh.''

''So I suggest you get your cute little fanny up and into the bathroom before we do something we'll both regret.''

''Speak for yourself.'' She didn't budge. ''You had second thoughts, huh?''

''Didn't you?''

She got out of bed, but then stopped at the bathroom door. ''How are you going to make contact with your friend?''

''This afternoon we have another in-your-face session. I'll pretend to get steamed again and take another ride to cool off.''

Cassie grimaced. ''I forgot about the group session. Maybe we should practice.''

He knew she was thinking about how he'd gone off before. ''Tell you what, this time you take the lead and I'll follow whatever avenue you take.''

''I still don't know what to say.''

''Whatever the topic is, express your own opinions if that's easier. I'll ad-lib from there.''

''Hope it doesn't end up being too hot a topic.''

''Don't worry.'' He sighed. ''No more surprises.''

She started to enter the bathroom but then hesitated. ''Dalton?''

Dread filled every pore in his body. Her tentative tone said it all. She was about to ask a question he didn't want to answer. He wouldn't discuss his marriage or Linda. The past was the past. The end. "Yeah?"

She didn't react to his impersonal tone. "I have a confession to make, too. Dammit, but I'm starting to like you."

"I HEAR Y'ALL murmuring back there." Mary Jane's disposition was a little too chipper for Cassie's mood, even more so than usual. "Don't worry. We only have ten minutes more of hiking."

"Don't look so enthusiastic." Dalton nudged her with his elbow. "Exercise is good for you."

"I don't mind exercising. In fact, I actually enjoy working out. I just want to know what the hell we're doing in the middle of nowhere."

"Me, too," Zelda said, obviously having overheard. "This is ridiculous. It's getting frightfully hot and we still have to walk back yet."

"Amen. Maybe we ought to start back now." Cassie made a face at the back of Mary Jane's perky high-stepping. "Miss Sunshine probably won't even miss us."

Zelda's eyes lit with hope. "Are you serious?"

Cassie peered at the thicket of trees ahead of them. They'd already plodded down a dirt road, trampled over shrubbery tall enough to scratch her legs and had to dodge two large tumbleweeds. As green as the grounds were at Back to Basics, the surrounding area was arid and undeveloped.

"I'm game," she said, thinking she could do some

more snooping around. "I'm pretty sure I know the way back."

"Honey…" Dalton took her arm. "You're the one who thought this week was such a good idea. I think we should stick with the program."

"But Zelda's right. What is this stupid hike going to prove?"

He didn't answer, but nor did he have to. She saw in his eyes that it was important that they stay with the group.

She gave Zelda an apologetic look. "Sorry, but I guess my husband is right. This was my idea."

"Well, this was my idea, too…the first time, anyway. But I'm sure sorry I ever met Mr. Blankenship." Zelda stopped to mop her face with a white linen handkerchief.

Cassie waited for her but waved Dalton on when he slowed. He nodded, probably realizing Zelda may be more open to talking alone with Cassie.

"Why do you say that?"

"I don't know." The older woman sighed. "He's got this way about him that makes it hard to say no."

"To what?"

Zelda's gaze flew to Cassie. "Not that. I mean nothing immoral, if that's what you're thinking." She lowered her voice and added, "Although my friend Maude and her husband attended the encounter week two months ago and she thought Mr. Blankenship had gotten awfully chummy with one of the other wives."

"Really?"

Zelda gave a smug nod.

"That's interesting." Cassie paused dramatically. "Do you think that's why he called Simone out of the dining room last night?"

Her features tightened. "Well, if he did, that one would be asking for it. I've already warned Harvey. He embarrasses me one more time with that tramp, and he'll be working for a living."

The wheels started to spin in Cassie's head. Maybe Simone *was* working with Bask and Mary Jane. Maybe that was Simone's job…to break up couples. "How did you hear about this place? Your friend Maude?"

"We really heard about it together. Robert…" She blinked, looking a little embarrassed before hurrying on, "that is, Mr. Blankenship, was at a charity ball we'd both attended and we overheard him talking to a couple about the success rate of the new program he'd started, about how couples benefited from strengthening the marriage bond. Maude loves trying every new wave cure that comes along so she signed up right away."

"How did it work for her?"

Zelda stopped to mop her forehead again, and Cassie waited with her. The others had already pulled way ahead, which was just fine because Cassie wasn't about to miss this opportunity to pump Zelda for information.

"I love Maude. I truly do. But the woman's a flake. She has too much money and too much time on her hands. Any distraction from life amuses her, so of course she loved the program."

They continued walking and Zelda added, "Though

I must say, Mr. Blankenship was able to accomplish something I haven't been able to do. I've told Maude over and over again that she should find a charity that interests her and get involved. She subscribes to the notion that writing a check is enough.''

She paused to catch her breath and impatient, Cassie said, ''And Blankenship has introduced her to a charity in which she's become involved.''

Zelda nodded. ''So I guess this particular distraction hasn't been all bad for Maude.''

''Hey, what's keeping you?'' Mary Jane called out with her hands cupped around her mouth.

''Wait until gravity and age gets a hold of that young lady.'' Zelda smiled. ''It couldn't happen to a more deserving person.''

Cassie laughed. ''You're usually so quiet. This is a new side to you. I like it.''

''The reason I haven't said much is because most of what comes to mind would be too undignified to verbalize.''

''I understand completely.'' They walked in companionable silence for the next minute, and then Cassie said, ''Would you mind if I asked you something personal?''

''Ask.'' Zelda gestured with her hand that it was all right. ''That's not to say I'll answer.''

Their conversation made Cassie all the more curious about the woman. She obviously wasn't some shrinking violet as it had first appeared. ''Why are you seeing the week through? Why don't you just leave?''

Zelda looked away and fidgeted with her ever-present braid.

"Robert thinks—" She stopped cold. "I guess I'm going to have to let that question remained unanswered."

"No problem," Cassie said breezily. "But if you have the chance to check with your friend, I'd really like to know about that charity she's working with. I may be interested myself."

"Oh, I don't need to check with Maude. I've decided to get involved, as well. It's called the R. Bask Scholarship Fund."

"Boy, have I got a lot to tell you," Cassie said under her breath to Dalton as the group gathered around a natural pool.

"I figured." He looked straight ahead, pretending to be listening to Mary Jane who seemed to be giving a canned speech about the pool and what it was used for in the old days. "She opened up, huh?"

"Yep. It's too hard to get into it now, but I think you'll be interested."

"Hell, dangle the carrot why don't you?"

Cassie grinned. "Just doing my job."

"I wouldn't drink the water," Mary Jane said, her voice rising as she looked pointedly at them. "But it's just deep enough to make a great swimming hole."

Dalton leaned his head toward Cassie. "Feels like we're back in school, doesn't it?"

"Shut up. She's giving us the eye again."

He smiled and straightened but didn't bother to pay

attention to Mary Jane. He kept thinking about Cassie, about how during the last fifteen minutes of the hike when she'd lagged behind with Zelda, he'd missed her like crazy.

Stupid, he knew, but it was the oddest feeling. He'd wanted her beside him, sharing a joke, exchanging observations, being able to inhale her private seductive scent. He had to remind himself of the spiel he'd given her. They were co-conspirators, and in a way now that he thought about it, they were almost like hostages, having to rely on each other for survival.

He knew better than to attach any more weight to their relationship or feelings for each other. It was all a temporary illusion. In fours days it would be over. He'd be sitting in a hotel room somewhere, writing his report, setting up Bask's arrest, and she'd be back settling into her own life.

Maybe they'd still keep in touch. But probably only on the phone. And only about the case. What more did they have in common, after all?

"In about an hour you'll eat the picnic lunches Tasha packed for each of you," Mary Jane was saying. "In the meantime I want you to go off in couples and scout the area. Find a place where you'll both feel comfortable."

"To eat our lunch?" Tom asked.

Mary Jane and Simone both laughed.

Grant produced a rare smile.

The rest of the group gave each other confused looks.

"This is our day in the wild," Mary Jane explained.

"A time to let our inhibitions go. To be comfortable with our bodies and our partners. To bring some of the spark and daring back into the romance.''

Dalton got the picture but it was obvious the others hadn't, including Cassie.

Mary Jane sighed. "To put it simply, you'll need a place to do the wild thing."

12

————————

"THIS HAS TO BE another ploy to get us out of the house again, don't you think?" Cassie crawled through the small crevice ahead of him and Dalton nearly fell on his face from keeping his eyes on her tempting backside instead of where he was stepping. "I mean who would think up something stupid like this?"

"Having a nature romp is stupid?"

"Well, I don't know... No, I guess not. But using it as a tool for marriage counseling? Come on."

"Mary Jane and Bask have both reminded us this isn't counseling. The answers are within us. We just have to dig," Dalton repeated Bask's words in a perfect imitation of his voice.

Cassie glanced over her shoulder. "You're downright spooky."

"This is far enough," he said when it looked as if she were about to climb another level of rocks.

"I don't want anyone to see us."

"Ah, so you plan on having your way with me, after all."

"What do you think the chances are, zero or nothing?" She glanced back at him again and caught him staring at her fanny. Quickly she turned her face. "I misspoke," she said, "I meant I didn't want anyone hearing us."

"Freudian slip, maybe."

"You are a dreamer." She plopped down on a flat surface. "I think this spot is good."

He settled in beside her. "So, tell me…"

"Tell you what?"

"Have you ever done the wild thing in the wild?"

She gave him an admonishing frown. "How is that your business?"

"Didn't say it was."

"You're annoying, you know that?"

"And here you said you were just beginning to like me."

A smile played at the corners of her mouth. "I lied." She opened the sack he'd snitched from Mary Jane. "Sandwiches and chips. Wow, real aphrodisiacs." She inspected the wrapped sandwiches closer. "You want turkey or ham?"

He was suddenly struck by the sun shining on her face, making her prefect skin even more luminous. Her lips were perfectly shaped, naturally tinted a pale pink. Screw lunch. He wondered what she'd say if he told her that he wanted her. Right now. Naked. Her legs parted so he could taste her.

Quickly he uncapped his water bottle and took a long cool sip, and then splashed some of it on his face.

"If you don't answer I'm sticking you with the ham."

He used the back of his rolled up sleeve to wipe his face. "Ham's fine."

"Too much sodium." She handed him the sandwich. "I hope you don't normally eat a lot of it."

"No, ma'am."

She looked up and tried to hide a smile. "It doesn't
hurt to have good nutrition."

"No, it doesn't," he agreed. "And a night of hot
sex works wonders, too."

Her lips parted in surprise. "Don't start. We
agreed."

He set down the sandwich and kissed her. She stiffened, but he guessed mostly because he'd caught her
off guard since she quickly molded herself against him
and returned the kiss with enthusiasm.

She clung to his shoulder as he lay back, bringing
her with him. Too many rocks made it uncomfortable
to stay in that position, but he didn't budge, enjoying
the weight of her breasts on his chest too much to care.

When they finally both came up for air, she laughed
softly. "I thought we were supposed to be having second thoughts."

"Yeah, I know. Trouble is, I'm in bad shape,
honey."

She lifted herself off him and wouldn't cooperate
when he tried to bring her back. "What do you
mean?"

"I've got you on the brain. All those wicked
thoughts are slugging it out with the second thoughts.
They're making me crazy."

She laughed and sank back against him.

"Thanks for your concern."

Her smile broadened as her hand traveled toward

his fly. "I bet I could relieve some of the pressure of those wicked thoughts."

He intercepted her hand just in time. "I bet you can."

"Playing hard to get, huh?" Cassie wiggled her wrist to no avail. He kept a firm hold. "Anyway, I figure I'm safe out here."

He stared at her a moment, waiting for the telltale smile, or mischievous twinkle in her eye. She wasn't kidding. "My, my, but you've lived a sheltered life."

"I have not."

"What makes you think you're safe out here?"

"Because it's too—it wouldn't be—would you please let go of me?"

"Would you please not change the subject? I'm genuinely interested in your opinion about outdoor...sports."

"You should be more interested in what I found out from Zelda."

"Touché." He let her go, and she made a show of rubbing her wrist. Hell, he hadn't held her that hard. She obviously didn't want to talk about outdoor sex, which made him all the more interested in the subject. And determined. "However, in my defense, I did figure that if you'd gotten anything significant out of her, you would have blurted it out by now."

"I don't blurt, and I did find out something important, if you care to hear it."

Dalton sighed. He'd done it again. Allowed his thoughts to get sidetracked. "Let's hear it."

She relayed her conversation with Zelda, impressing

him with her terrific memory. She hit the high points, remembered names and time frames, most of it interesting, though not a lot they didn't already know or could use. Except now he knew to keep an eye on Zelda. He hadn't figured her for a candidate but the way Cassie described her weird kind of fascination or reverence for Bask, that made her vulnerable.

"Oh, and the pièce de résistance." She looked pleased with herself. "Did you know that Bask operates a charity?"

"A charity, as in soliciting donors?"

She nodded. "Guess what he calls it."

"I hope that question is rhetorical."

Cassie smiled. "The R. Bask Scholarship Fund."

Dalton drew his head back. "Son of a bitch. What's he doing, funding the next generation of crooks?"

"I don't know, but he's got people working the fund and contributing."

"I'll be damned." Nothing in his file indicated that kind of information. "Any idea when he came up with that particular brainchild?"

"At least two or three months ago according to what Zelda told me. But I could probably find out more. I did tell her I might be interested in volunteering so it wouldn't seem odd if I had more questions."

"Hold off for now." He lapsed into thought while Cassie unwrapped her sandwich.

"Here." She offered him half.

"What happened to mine?"

"It's right here, a ton of sodium along with it." She

chuckled when he looked skyward in disgust. "Let's each have half the ham and half the turkey."

"But you wanted the turkey."

She shrugged, looking embarrassed suddenly. "Yeah, but I don't want you croaking on me. Just eat the damn half a turkey, okay?"

"Knock it off, Cass, or I'm going to start thinking you care." He accepted the sandwich, and gave her a teasing grin in return. But damn if his heart wasn't pounding like crazy.

A SHRILL WHISTLE split the silence. Mary Jane's signal that it was time to regroup and head back. Cassie slowly opened her eyes to clear blue sky. She caught Dalton out of the corner of her eye just as another blow of the whistle sent birds flying everywhere.

Amazingly he still slept. The whistle hadn't fazed him.

She hated to wake him. They'd both had too little sleep in the past three nights. But if she didn't, Mary Jane was sure to send the hounds after them.

"Dalton?" Cassie touched his shoulder. "Dalton, you have to get up."

He murmured something incoherent and then rolled onto his side.

Cassie inched closer and molded herself to him spoon fashion, her mouth close to his ear. "Dalton, if you don't get up I'm leaving you here."

He groaned and stretched his neck, but wouldn't open his eyes.

"Come on, Dalton." She brushed aside the hair

from the back of his neck and was tempted to plant several small kisses there. "Wake up, sleepyhead."

"Is it time to go?" he muttered.

"Yep." Taking advantage of his dazed state, she put her arms around him and pressed her breasts against his back. He was so broad and strong, and he felt too damn good.

He yawned, and reached a hand around to cup her bottom. The move seemed so familiar and comfortable it made her shiver.

Mary Jane let out another ear-splitting whistle. It seemed closer this time.

"Shit. I'm going to take that thing and wrap it around her neck."

"I'll help." Cassie made no move to get up. The sun's warmth and still feeling a little drowsy herself, made her want to wrap herself around Dalton and stay just as they were until the sun set.

"I can't believe I dozed off."

"I can. We both needed the sleep."

"You fell asleep, too?" He twisted around to look at her.

She nodded. "A second after you did." Not quite true. She'd stayed awake a while, turning over all of the details of the case in her mind.

Dalton didn't say anything more. Just kept staring at her.

"What?"

"You are so beautiful."

"Dalton, are you high?" She pulled away and scrambled to her feet.

"Nope. I haven't been high in ten years." He got up and dusted his hands together. "Don't tell me you aren't used to men telling you that all the time."

"Of course not." She didn't get flustered often but he'd really taken her by surprise. "Don't just stand there, grab that bag of trash and your water bottle."

"Yes, ma'am."

She set her own water bottle aside and pulled off her T-shirt.

His boots skidded on the rocks as his gaze riveted to her blue-silk-covered breasts. "What are you doing?"

"Nothing exciting, believe me." She turned the T-shirt inside out.

"You worry about sodium in my diet and then try to give me a friggin' heart attack."

"Oh, please, how many women have you seen in a bra before?" She pulled the shirt back on, inside out.

"Probably a couple hundred or more."

She slid him a sideways glance as she retrieved her water bottle.

He grinned. "But none of them as beautiful as you."

She shook her head. "You're starting to sound as slippery as Bask."

"Low blow. And here I was about to compliment you on your new fashion statement." He paused and gave her a considering look. "Actually, pretty good thinking."

"Mary Jane kept turning around and eyeing Zelda and me. I doubt she thought we were doing anything other than idly chatting, but it won't hurt for her to think we'd followed her instructions.''

''And were so involved, we had to dress quickly.''

''Exactly.''

''Nice touch.''

''Thank you.''

''By the way, I like that bra you're wearing.'' He followed her down the slope. ''The color suits you.''

She laughed. ''You're a piece of work.'' A sudden sharp incline made her move faster. She got to where it was level again and turned to wait for him. ''Let's hope Bask agrees with you.''

Dalton frowned. ''About your bra?''

Slowly she nodded. ''I made an appointment for a private counseling session with him tomorrow night.''

''YOU'RE TOO UPTIGHT.'' Harvey and Zelda faced each other in the front of the room later that afternoon while the rest of the group observed without interrupting. ''Too worried about what's proper and how it will be construed,'' Harvey said, his tone more resigned than angry.

''You don't understand my social position. You never have.'' Zelda spoke softly, reluctantly. Occasionally her gaze would stray toward Bask, who'd give her a reassuring nod. ''My family name has a certain responsibility attached to it.''

''I'm not talking about social situations. I'm talking about us. In the bedroom.''

Zelda drew back, crossing her arms protectively against her chest. ''That's not what this discussion is

supposed to be about," she whispered, her gaze going
again to Bask, who remained stone-faced.

"Of course it is," Harvey said. "It's about everything that has to do with a healthy marriage."

Zelda sat in silence, a flush crawling up her neck.

Everyone else in the room was so quiet you could
hear a pin drop. Dalton glanced at Cassie. She sat
spellbound by the drama unfolding. Empathy was all
over her face and he felt a tug in his gut he didn't want
to analyze.

"I just wish—" Harvey passed an agitated hand
down his face. "I wish you were more adventurous
like Simone."

Zelda's arms fell to her side, and her eyes blazed
with hurt and anger. "Don't you dare compare me to
anyone else. Especially not to that...woman."

The way she said *woman* pretty much let everyone
know what she thought of Simone. But in a much more
subtle, dignified way the rich seemed to have down
pat. Still, Dalton felt for the older woman. That someone as refined and genteel as her could be manipulated
by Bask made him despise the guy all the more.

"I'm sorry," Harvey said gently, reaching for her
hand. "You're absolutely right. I didn't mean to hurt
your feelings. I only meant—"

Dalton cringed. Didn't the guy know when to shut
up?

"Never mind. Please accept my apology." Harvey
kissed her hand, and Zelda relaxed a little. She still
didn't seem too pleased but at least she stayed put and

listened patiently as, with Bask's coaching, Harvey continued.

The whole thing was giving Dalton a headache. Hell, relationships were too damn complicated. But Zelda and Harvey weren't his problem, and he was a fool for investing so much as an emotional second in them. He strove for simplicity. In the relationship department, he had no problem. No wife. No complications. He liked his life that way. This retreat just proved he was right.

His gaze went involuntarily to Cassie. She watched the couple from the edge of her chair, her heart on her sleeve.

She was a rookie. She'd learn not to become emotionally involved.

After another ten minutes of listening to Harvey and Zelda beat a dead horse, Bask stood and hugged both of them. Dalton snorted. If Bask tried hugging him, he'd need a plastic surgeon real quick.

"You did great," he said in that smooth oily voice of his. "Did you notice how your tones changed toward the end?" He looked out at the group. "Did you all hear it?" Kathy was the only one who nodded. "It means you're starting to learn to refine your communication, be more respectful of the other person. You did a fine job." He motioned for them to reclaim their seats in the audience.

They'd gone first, no telling who'd be called up next. Dalton hunched down and avoided eye contact with Bask.

"Let's see." Bask's gaze scanned the group. "How about if we hear from Dalton and Cassie next?"

"Shit."

Cassie shot him a disapproving look as she left her chair. No one else apparently heard him. He pushed himself up, preferring a root canal to what he was about to go through.

As he approached the appointed chair, Bask gave him an encouraging smile that Dalton wanted to smash off his face.

They sat down and faced each other just as Zelda and Harvey had done. Cassie seemed nervous, too. Or maybe it was an act. She amazed him with her poise and wit under pressure.

Someone had noticed Cassie's shirt being inside out right away that afternoon, and they both took some good-natured ribbing all the way back to the house. He had to admit, she was good. Sometimes it was the little details that made or broke a case.

"Who would like to start?" Bask asked when neither of them uttered a word.

Cassie moistened her lips but didn't volunteer.

Dalton cleared his throat. "I think Cassie should go first since the last time I left abruptly without giving her a chance."

She narrowed her gaze just enough for him to get the hint. She was going to strangle him later.

"Cassie." Bask gestured to her and then reclaimed his seat off to the right.

"Okay." She took a deep breath, and then stared

blankly for a moment. "Let's see…" She took another deep breath and then froze.

"Maybe I can help you out here," Bask said, his voice calm, soothing…annoying as hell. "Why don't you start where Dalton left off?"

Dalton groaned. "I thought that subject had been put to rest."

"Cassie hasn't had her chance at rebuttal, if you will." Bask clasped his hands together and sat back. "Cassie, go ahead."

Dalton sank down and hunched his shoulders, and stared at his outstretched legs. Shit. At least he wouldn't forget what the story was.

"Dalton? I think it would be better if you looked at me."

Slowly he lifted his gaze. She looked serious. Too serious. She'd better damn well better remember this was playacting.

"I'm glad we're starting at this point. I have to admit, what you said yesterday has been bothering me."

She wanted eye contact? She got it. He stared intensely into her eyes, trying to get the warning across. Anything she said was not really supposed to be about him. He silently willed her to stick with their act.

"Marriage is a partnership," she said, "at least that's the way I see it. The way I want my marriage to work. It's not solely up to you to provide for me, or our eventual family. We need to do it together."

She blinked, and then stared down at her hands. "I'm not just a hood ornament, incapable of being anything except decoration."

"Cassie, keep eye contact with Dalton," Bask said quietly.

She stiffened but lifted her chin. The earnestness in her eyes made Dalton's chest tighten. "It's not about money or ego or anything else," she said softly. "It's about two people respecting and trusting each other enough to share the responsibility of making a marriage work, the responsibility of earning and managing money in order to raise a family. It's being a shoulder to lean on or cry on when the road gets rocky."

After an uncomfortable silence, Dalton said, "Easier said than done."

"Trite but true." Cassie lips curved a little. "Sometimes it's really hard to push bias and ego aside. But when you do, the bond strengthens. We become a team. And when the next crisis or disagreement arises, it's easier to overcome."

"You're doing great, really terrific," Bask said, "but try to get specific, Cassie, so Dalton fully understands how this all pertains to him."

"I'm sure he knows what I'm talking about," she mumbled.

"Come on, Cassie, don't backpedal now," Bask urged, his voice becoming more hypnotic. "You're making progress. I can see it on Dalton's face."

Right. Dalton bit back a remark and consoled himself with the satisfying thought of arresting Bask's ass. If they couldn't dig up anything to give a prosecutor soon, they could at least put him behind bars for passing himself off as a marriage counselor without a license, while they dug deeper.

He just hoped Cassie remembered that this therapy stuff was bullshit, that what she was saying didn't apply to him. He watched anxiety build in her eyes as she mentally prepared herself for the next round.

"I don't want to be in competition with your job, whether it be charity work or managing our portfolio."

Good girl. He relaxed.

"Nor do I want your job to compete against me. There are times when a deadline or a project will keep you busy for hours, maybe even days, or a week. I understand. The same applies to me. I may not be able to give you the attention you want all the time. But that doesn't mean the connection is gone. It doesn't mean I won't be waiting for you with open arms. You can be a good husband, and eventually father, and still be a good breadwinner, too."

Dalton stared at her with mistrust. He knew she'd checked him out, but had she somehow gotten into his personal file? Nah, it wouldn't matter. This kind of stuff wasn't in there. But how could she hit so close to home?

"You're still not being specific, Cassie," Bask admonished.

Dalton stood. "This is bullshit," he said and in a replay of the last session, headed for the door

But unlike yesterday, Simone burst into tears and ran out ahead of him.

13

DALTON TRIED Frank's cell phone number. Four-fifteen. The old buzzard was probably taking a break at Mario's coffee and doughnut shop. Dalton hoped so. It would be easier for Frank to talk about anything he might have found outside of the office.

As the phone rang, Dalton's thoughts went back to Cassie and the therapy session. Some cooling off time away from her had cleared his head some and he realized now that she couldn't have known she'd hit on his and Linda's main problem.

Cassie might have guessed from the last session or from parts of their private conversations, but the earnestness in her eyes made him think her words were more from the heart, possibly from her own experience.

"Frank here."

He adjusted the phone to his mouth. "It's me. Find out anything?"

"Other than the fact that Higgins is so pissed at you he's probably arranging to transfer you to Outer Mongolia?"

"Screw Higgins." Dalton rubbed his tired eyes. "What did you find out?"

"Simone Harding has a list of aliases a mile long. She's been Adele Manning, Sandra Lockhart, Danielle Fleming, Morgan Sanders... Any of these sound familiar?"

"Not off hand. Any arrests?"

"Two, both times for fraud, but no convictions."

"What about Grant Harding?"

"Not a thing on him."

That didn't mean anything, but somehow Dalton wasn't surprised. He doubted there was any relationship between Grant and Simone. Grant had probably been hired to pose as her husband, and it was possible that he didn't know about Bask's scam.

Hell, it was possible Bask didn't even know about Simone.

She could have her own private agenda, her own scam in the works. No, it was that hint of familiarity the evening Bask had called her out of the dining room that had gotten Dalton thinking. "Have Bask and Simone ever been linked together?"

"Funny you should ask. Simone was last seen in Wichita, Kansas. Same place your boy, Bask, was taken in for questioning two years ago."

"Makes sense," Dalton muttered, and then listened while Frank filled him in on a few more items of interest.

Now that they knew Simone was involved somehow, Dalton figured she would be the better person to lean on. The heavy drinking could be an act, but he didn't think so. She seemed to always be sober, yet no one consumed as much alcohol as she did and not get sloshed. Yep, she was ripe for the picking.

"Thanks, Frank. I owe you one."

"One?" Frank chuckled. "You owe me more than one, pal."

"Yeah, you're right."

"Hey, aren't you gonna ask why you're in the doghouse with Higgins?"

"Shit, when am I not in the doghouse with him?"

"Yeah, but it's different this time." Frank's voice got serious. "You haven't checked in for almost a week, and he's been alternating between worried and furious."

"He's worried about me? Wait while I wipe a tear."

Frank laughed. "You know it wouldn't look good if he lost a man right before election time."

"So he's really going to run for office?"

"Looks like it."

Dalton shook his head. Part of him wished the guy got elected so he'd get off his back, and the other part missed the pain in the ass already.

They'd worked together a long time. While Dalton had liked staying out in the field, Hector had higher aspirations. He'd been promoted rather quickly, and with each promotion he'd changed, became more ambitious. "I assume he asked if you heard from me?"

"Yeah…wait a minute." Frank pulled away from the phone and said, "Honey, a little more coffee here."

Yep, he was at Mario's, all right. Some things never

changed. Dalton smiled. Including Frank's political incorrectness.

"Okay," Frank said into the receiver. "I told him I hadn't talked to you since last week."

"Good. I don't want you in the middle."

"Why haven't you checked in?"

"I left a message."

"A week ago. On his voice mail when you knew he wouldn't be in."

"So?"

"I hate to say it, kid, but it looks like you're purposely trying to piss him off."

"He stuck me with this friggin' nothing case. If he doesn't like the way I'm working it, he can pull me off." As soon as the words were out of his mouth, realization hit him like a two-by-four.

If Higgins had known Dalton had planned to go undercover, he *would* have pulled him off, and sent someone else. Higgins didn't really want Dalton wasting his time on this kind of case. He'd only wanted to exact punishment, make an example out of him.

"He can't pull you off if he doesn't hear from you."

Exactly. Dalton briefly closed his eyes and muttered a pithy four-letter word. This was about Cassie, and wanting to work with her. Hell, wanting to do more than work with her. He knew better. Dammit.

"Dalton?"

"I'm here."

"Just check in. You don't even have to tell him where you are."

"Yeah, you're probably right."

Frank sighed. "That sounded a lot like Marie's 'yes, dear.' I still think you should call."

"Thanks, Frank. When I get back I'm taking you and Marie to dinner."

"If you aren't standing in the unemployment line instead."

"Hell, I need a vacation, anyway."

"Right."

"See ya."

Dalton stood at the payphone, drumming his fingers on the ratty phonebook stored beneath the phone. In spite of their recent differences, Higgins probably was worried.

"Shit!"

He picked up the receiver again and punched in the number to the bureau. Purposely he didn't call Higgins's private line. When the operator answered, he asked for Higgins's assistant. And left a message.

"LET'S TAKE A WALK." Dalton steered Cassie to the French doors as soon as dinner was over.

Cassie glanced over her shoulder. "It's such a nice evening, someone else is bound to have the same idea."

"Nah, they're all tired from their hike this morning."

She hoped so. She was dying to talk to him and would have preferred the privacy of their room. But she followed him out onto the patio, and the scent of roses and gardenias immediately surrounded them. A couple of rakes leaned against a post, which meant the gardener hadn't left yet.

"Let's head toward the pool," Dalton said, and surprised her by taking her hand.

She inhaled deeply. "These roses are awesome. I'm really going to have to talk to Mr. Hamada."

"You were serious about that?"

"Of course. I love to garden."

"Yeah, that's right. You said something about that in the car."

"You look skeptical."

"I don't know. I just didn't see you as the type."

She frowned. Surely he didn't think she was afraid to get her hands dirty. "I'm not sure how to take that."

"I see you more as a career woman, not someone tinkering around the house or yard, or fooling with girlie things."

"Oh." She smiled, liking that answer.

He gave her a double take, and smiled along with her. "What's that sassy grin for?"

"I don't usually get that response. Most people expect someone who looks like me to do girlie things."

He made a face as if he found that hard to believe. "Not people who know you."

She nodded wryly. "My father for one, and my mother to some degree. My brother, too, which really disappoints me because he's too young to have such a crummy attitude, and of course, my old boss was a member of the idiot society."

"Chet?"

She nodded, surprised he remembered Chet's name.

"I had a couple of old boyfriends like that, too, but I got rid of them fast."

He chuckled. "I bet you did." He lapsed into a thoughtful silence until they got to the pool deck. "Your parents are the ones who surprise me. Obviously I don't know them but I'd think they'd want you to strive for your full potential."

"One would think." She let go of his hand and sat on one of the lounge chairs, not sure she wanted to have this conversation. Her parents' lack of support in her career choice was a sore issue for her.

"You went to Texas A&M, not a scrub school. Did they encourage you to go?"

She shrugged. "Yeah, but only for my pageant portfolios."

God, she hoped she didn't regret supplying that information.

He sat beside her instead of on his own chair. "As in beauty pageants?"

She nodded already deep in regret.

"I can't picture it. I mean, you're certainly beautiful enough, I bet you won more than your share of competitions, but it just doesn't seem like you."

"Really?"

"Don't take it wrong or anything."

Laughing, she threw her arms around his neck. "Trust me, I am not taking this wrong," she said, and kissed him. Catching him off guard, he fell backward against the reclining chair back, pulling her with him. What was meant to be a for-show kiss quickly escalated. His warm chocolate-scented breath mixed with hers, and she let her weight rest against him, reveling in his instant arousal.

He framed her face with his hands and pushed her hair off her face, showering her with kisses. "God, you smell good."

"Wake up. It's garlic. The same thing you had for dinner," she joked, hoping to lighten the mood. She took a quick look around. Mostly to get her heart rate under control. "You're supposed to tell me about what you found out from your friend."

"Oh, hell, how am I supposed to remember right now?"

She looked down into his eyes, so full of humor and intelligence, and she knew that as impossible as it seemed, she'd fallen for him. She used the tip of her finger to trace the outline of his lips. "What happened to business before pleasure?"

"That's a bunch of bullshit." His lips curved and then he sucked her finger into his mouth.

"Hey, knock it off."

He bit down gently, just enough to get her revved.

She retaliated with a strategic little shimmy, making him groan.

"Ah, so the gloves are off, huh?" He grabbed her wrists and held them over her head.

"Dalton, let me go." She used a horrified voice, but then lost ground by laughing when he used his chin to tickle her neck.

"Not until you tell me you're crazy about me."

"In this lifetime?" She took an unsteady breath. She was acting like a rookie. "Not."

Dalton's grin vanished and he jerked his head up. "Did you hear something?"

"No." She sat up and stared into the semidarkness, neither of them speaking for nearly a minute.

He sat up, as well. "Could have been a cat or a bird."

"Or Mr. Hamada."

"It's getting too dark for him to still be working."

Shivering, she wrapped her arms around herself, thinking about how someone could have been watching them.

Dalton got up first and extended a hand. "Let's go inside."

She let him pull her up and then take her hand. He led her through the portion of the path that was a tad overgrown, and then brought her beside him, slipping an arm around her shoulders.

She liked the way they fit, the way he touched her without crowding her, how he had a kind of protective, chivalrous streak. She'd never admit it to him. They were professional, equals, and she wanted desperately to be taken seriously. Anyway, he'd deny it. He'd probably start second-guessing his actions, not wanting to appear soft.

Snuggled against him, she whispered, "Tell me about your childhood."

"Why?"

"I want to know about you."

"We've been in each other's face for three days. I think you're starting to get to know me."

"That's not fair. I told you about my parents and the beauty pageants."

He sighed. "Can we talk about this later so we aren't overheard? We're supposed to know all this stuff about each other. We're married, remember?"

She didn't say anything. He was right except she got the feeling he was putting her off. Finally, she said, "Just one thing and I promise to shut up."

"Right." One side of his mouth lifted. "What?"

"Did you have an awful childhood?"

He drew his head back. "Why would you ask that?"

"Because you don't want to talk about it, and if that's the case, that's fine, I understand, but I really want to know."

"You couldn't be further off the mark. Very normal. Both parents in the house—Dad worked, and Mom stayed at home. My brother and I were raised with a strong hand and even stronger work ethic. So, no, you don't have to call a shrink for me."

"I'd guessed you had a good upbringing. You're very courteous and—"

"I thought you were going to shut up."

She jabbed him with her elbow. "Did I say courteous?"

He grunted on impact. "You know we could keep walking, maybe down the driveway. It's open and we can talk."

"It's also getting too dark." Disappointment pricked her. "It sounds like you're trying to avoid me again."

"Not true. I just want to hurry and get the business part out of the way."

"Oh."

He stopped and picked a rose. There was a mass of the blooms, so she didn't protest. He didn't give it to her as she expected him to, but took it into the house with them.

A light was on in the kitchen and the usual dim lamp shone in the parlor, but the house was quiet, the downstairs apparently deserted.

Silently they went up to their room and Dalton locked the door behind them. Cassie's pulse picked up speed when he turned to look at her.

He held up the pinkish-melon-colored rose, stared at it for a second and then his gaze went back to her. "This is the exact color of your lips."

Her hand went to her mouth self-consciously. "But I don't even have on any lipstick."

"I know. This is the way you look when you wake up in the morning."

Heat flooded her cheeks at the thought of him watching her as she awoke. Foolish, really, since they'd already spent three nights together. "Hurry up and tell me what you found out from your friend."

Dalton smiled. "Mostly what we already suspected. It looks as if Simone's working with Bask."

She took the rose from him and got some water. "How did you find out?"

"She's got a string of aliases so she's not exactly the model citizen, and she's been seen in the same cities at the same time with Bask."

"But they've never been arrested together?"

"Nope. Of course Bask is so damn sly he should've been arrested twenty times but hasn't."

"Simone isn't." Cassie couldn't help but feel some pity for the woman. "She's a mess."

"Oh, yeah. What happened with her after I left?"

"Nothing, really. The session went on without the two of you."

"You should try and talk to her again. Maybe she'll either be down or drunk enough to say something."

"I tried. I ran after her, but Bask broke us up in a heartbeat. Sent me back to the session and then showed up, alone, five minutes later."

Dalton's lips lifted in a slow smile and he gave her that look again, the one that said "nice work." "Maybe tomorrow you'll have another opportunity."

"Heck, I'll make one." She frowned. "What about Grant? Is he really her husband?"

"Doesn't look like it. But she needs one to be here so he's probably just a hired flunky."

"Geez, she could have at least found someone she had some chemistry with. The way those two interact gives me the creeps."

He frowned. "Why?"

"Please. Married people don't act that way."

"Many of them do."

"Then they shouldn't be married." She saw the smirk lurking at the corners of his mouth, and she could tell he thought she was being naive just because she hadn't been married. Tough. "Mary Jane still puzzles me. Simone's job is obviously to stir up trouble between the couples, but how does Mary Jane fit in?''

''I don't know. Maybe she's clean. Simply hired help like the cook and gardener.''

''Maybe. Of course she does a little stirring herself.''

''Hell, she's too annoying to get the husbands excited.''

Cassie looked at him in disbelief. ''Right. You almost got whiplash trying to check out her thong.''

''I did not.''

''The hell you didn't.''

He grinned. ''Jealous?''

She lifted her chin. ''That'll be the day.''

''Guess what?'' He reached for her hand.

Her pulse went bananas again. ''What?''

''Business is over,'' he said, and captured her mouth with a demanding kiss.

14

DALTON TASTED her excitement and fear. Not fear of him; fear that something big was happening between them, something much bigger than sex. And he knew that he was a damn fool to take this relationship further.

But he couldn't help himself. More and more she consumed his thoughts. Never had he been so distracted from a case. Good thing it was a no-brainer assignment. In truth, had he been diligent he could have probably wrapped things up already.

He couldn't think about that now, though, not when Cassie was warm and soft and opening her mouth to him. She made a whimpering sound that sparked an urgency in him, and he guided her backward toward the bed.

She immediately unbuttoned his shirt and before they got to the bed, he pulled her T-shirt over her head. Her bra was red, silky and left little to the imagination. He quickly undid the front clasp and filled his palms with her soft satiny flesh.

Arching her head back, she moaned softly. ''Dalton, take your clothes off,'' she whispered feverishly. ''All of them.''

He dipped his head to take a nipple into his mouth and suckled it slowly, fighting the impulse to lie her down, pull off her jeans and spread her thighs. He wanted to taste her, be inside her, to make her scream when she came.

"Dalton, I want you inside me." Her whisper melted him like butter.

She reached for his buckle and disposed of his belt in seconds. Another second and she unzipped his fly. Afraid that she'd touch him and everything would happen too quickly, he ended up confused when she didn't even try to pull off his jeans.

Instead, she ran her finger across his belly, over the skin above his waistband. Every time it felt as if she might dip into his open fly, she ran her flattened palm up to his chest. And then he saw the sly smile tugging at the corners of her mouth and knew she was purposely teasing him.

This time, the gloves came off.

Cassie swallowed. Not because she was nervous. But excited. Impossibly turned on. It wasn't just his touch that had her pulse skidding out of control, but the hungry look in his eyes....

He unsnapped, unzipped and pulled down her rose-colored jeans before she finished gasping. When she didn't readily step out of the jeans, he lifted one ankle out of the slim-fitting leg, and then the other. Her thong matched the red silk bra he'd thrown on the armoire, and he reached around, cupping her bottom with both hands.

He sat on the edge of the mattress, spread his legs

into a vee and pulled her between them. Just when she thought he'd take one of her breasts into his mouth, he slowly turned her around.

At first she resisted, staring at him with a puzzled look, but she let him have his way. Either she trusted him or she didn't.

"I just want to look at you," he said, as if sensing her uncertainty.

He pulled her back toward him. "You're something else, lady. You're beautiful...perfect..." The words died and he just stared at her.

"What?" She tried to skitter away.

"Don't." He didn't restrain her.

She glanced over her shoulder at him. She wanted to bolt, but she wanted to stay. He made the decision by bracketing the sides of her thighs to hold her steady, and then kissing each soft cheek. He bit one lightly and she tensed her muscles. He licked the spot.

"Take off your panties."

She tensed again, hesitated, but then hooked her fingers into the elastic.

"No, don't turn around yet." He continued to grip her thighs when she tried to face him. "Take off the panties first."

Again she hesitated, but only for a moment, and then she slowly slid the red silk down her thighs, bending at the waist as she guided the panties down her calves.

She heard his sharp intake of breath. His reaction gave her courage and she moved to the music in her head. Warm breath fanned her skin. His mouth. Close. Her heart nearly exploded.

She wanted to turn around. See his expression. She wanted to feel his mouth on her.

He moved his hands from her thighs and ran them over her buttocks, and she immediately started to straighten. "Wait, baby."

Lightly he squeezed her flesh, then slid his hands to open her thighs, using his thumbs to find her damp core. She whimpered when he reached the thick thatch of curls and jerked back toward him. He inserted a finger inside her. She whimpered again, clenching her muscles around him and stood upright.

He withdrew his finger and let her turn around. Heat seared her face, but she met his glittering eyes, put her hands on his shoulders. He hauled her closer and drew one of her nipples into his mouth.

She pulled away before she shattered in a thousand pieces. "Take off your jeans."

He smiled at her admonishing tone.

She stepped back to show him she meant it. "Now."

He didn't respond right away, but let his gaze roam over one breasts and then the other until she wasn't sure who was in charge. Finally, he did as she asked, slowly, shoving his jeans to his hips, watching her watch him.

She blatantly stared as he lifted his hips and pushed the jeans down his legs, and then kicked them aside. His erection strained against the black boxers, but he didn't remove them, but waited for her instructions.

"Keep going," she said, her gaze stayed riveted to the way his boxers tented, gesturing impatiently when he didn't respond right away. "The boxers."

"Yes, ma'am." He smiled and pulled them off.

Incredible. He stole her breath.

She reached out and used the tip of her forefinger to touch the bead of moisture at the end of his arousal.

"That might be a little dangerous." He grabbed her wrist, stopping her and guiding her to the bed, forcing her to sit down.

"Hey, I'm calling the shots—" she said, her voice ending in a muffled groan when his mouth captured hers.

He laid her back, running his hands up her belly to her breasts, kneading and stroking while his tongue explored her mouth. She managed to get hold of him and he froze.

"You have to stop."

She stroked him again, really getting into the rhythm this time.

He groaned and grabbed her wrist. She tried to resist, but he caught her other hand, brought her wrists together and held them together with one hand. She yanked and twisted and almost got free.

He nibbled her lower lip. "Don't make me tie you up."

"Knock it off. You're getting me excited."

He drew back to look at her, uncertain about her teasing. A hopeful glint lit his eyes. "You mean we might have a use for my handcuffs?"

She laughed. "Maybe another time."

He blinked, and she didn't miss the hint of misgiving in his eyes. What? All she'd said was another time. It wasn't as if she were asking for a future with him.

The idea rattled her.

"Well, now that you've got me," she said with a mischievous look meant to put him at ease. "Whatever are you going to do with me?"

A slowly sexy smile lifted his lips. "Shock that smirk off your face." With that, he traced his tongue softly across her throat to her collarbone, then slid down to suckle one nipple and then the other. He raised his head, pleased at her heavy breathing. "What would you *like* me to do with you?"

Her eyes had drifted closed and her lips parted but she said nothing.

"Maybe something like this?" He fluttered his free hand lower until he reached her opening and slid two fingers into her slick warm wetness.

"Dalton." She whimpered and tried to bring her thighs together. Too late. He'd staked his territory.

She was so damn wet. So ready. He was the one being teased and tortured. He wanted to be inside of her. Now.

"Dalton?" Her nails dug into the back of his hand. She groaned and arched her back. "Do you have condoms?"

He continued stroking her with his fingers. In his wallet, there had to be a couple.

"You'd better get them," she panted.

"I don't need them for what I'm doing." He trailed

the tip of his tongue down to her navel. "What I'm about to do..."

"Dalton, get those damn things now."

He laughed at the frustration in her voice. "Okay, baby, we have all night to get creative."

He released her and got up from the bed. Where the hell had he thrown his jeans?"

Cassie watched him dig into his pocket and pull out his wallet. She had never in her entire life been so turned on. If he didn't hurry, she was going to come just watching him. He had a hell of a great body, and his sexy smile turned her ability to reason to mashed potatoes. His backside was so firm and perfect it made her want to weep.

And the front...his...

She closed her eyes and tried to recall the words to "Mary Had a Little Lamb." No more teasing. She needed him inside her now. And she wasn't kidding. He'd have to save his creative energy for later. But right now...

"Hey, Sleeping Beauty."

She opened her eyes.

Dalton stood at the edge of the bed, his erection still at full mast. "You had me worried." He stretched out beside her. "I thought I'd put you to sleep."

She shivered at the intensity of his stare. She sure hoped she knew what she was doing. Shadowy feelings that went deeper than they should had haunted her all day. "Dalton?"

He cupped her cheek, using the pad of his thumb to

stroke her skin. His gaze stayed with hers as he waited for her to speak.

"I just wanted to say…that is, I want you to know that tonight is just tonight." She bit her lower lip. "Does that make sense?"

He hesitated, and then nodded. "Yes, Cassie. I understand."

Did he? His expression had shut down and she couldn't read him. "Kiss me," she said.

He angled his head and kissed her on the lips, not too lightly and not too hard. The song was right. It was in his kiss. Everything was okay with them.

When he finally pulled away, he asked, "Do you want to put this on me?"

She looked at the foil packet. "You do it."

He sat up, totally at ease with his body and state of arousal, and tore open the packet.

Just watching him touch himself got her so hot and bothered she feared she'd fall apart as soon as he touched her. He was obviously very skilled at making a woman happy.

"Cassie? You okay?"

She realized she'd been staring, her thoughts wandering. "Impatient, but okay."

His confident smile made her swallow hard. "Come here."

She got up on one elbow and leaned toward him.

He shook his head.

Unsure what to do she got up on her knees.

He shifted back a foot and piled both their pillows together behind his back. "Come."

She moved toward him, hoping he'd give her direction. As soon as she was within arm's length, he grabbed her waist and urged her to sit astride him. But he didn't guide himself into her as she thought he might. He cupped her face with both hands and kissed her, parting her lips with his tongue.

His hands moved to her shoulders and then to her breasts.

She reached for him and he jerked, breaking the kiss and trying to stop her from circling him.

She laughed softly. "This goes both ways, honey."

"Yeah, but you aren't ready to explode."

"Wanna bet?"

"Ah, Cassie." His breathing was ragged, his voice hoarse. "Baby, we better take it slow."

"Why?"

"Because…hell, I don't know."

She positioned herself and slid onto him.

He cried out. Or maybe it had been her. She had no idea.

She stayed motionless a moment, getting used to feel of him inside her. He felt so good, so right tears burned the back of her eyes.

When she finally moved, the earth shifted with her.

DALTON LAY BESIDE Cassie, playing with a strand of her hair while she slept. A slim stream of light coming from the bathroom shone on the right side of her face.

After making love three times, in three different positions, she'd completely worn him out. He had no idea why he wasn't sound asleep. He should be. Instead of doing what he had no business doing—thinking about after the case. About reasons why he should still see her. Hell, how he could see her.

His job would likely take care of the problem. He traveled so damn much, at least three different cities a month, requiring stays anywhere from one to three weeks.

He liked that about his job. Travel prevented monotony. Kept him out of the office. Away from Higgins and the other suits who made Dalton nuts with their political ambitions and kiss-ass hierarchy and by-the-book preaching. Let them get out in the field and have to live by the letter of the law.

Many of the higher-ups had once been field agents. Caught up in the agency's politics, they'd forgotten that sometimes survival meant you lived by your wits, that there was no neat and tidy rule that would get you out of a tight spot. Especially one that was life-threatening.

Higgins thought Dalton was the one who was nuts. With his Princeton education and excellent arrest record, Dalton knew he could quickly climb the ranks within the bureau. He simply wasn't interested.

His parents didn't understand either. Especially his father who thought Dalton should have a loftier goal. At least they hadn't paid for his education so they couldn't claim their money had been wasted. He'd had a full ride, every penny of his tuition had come from either a scholarship or grant.

At one point he'd almost done it, taken a desk job to make Linda happy. But when push came to shove, he couldn't cave in. How happy could he have made her if he was miserable?

"Dalton?"

Cassie's sleepy voice penetrated his thoughts. He let go of her hair. "Sorry, honey, did I wake you?"

She turned onto her side and slipped an arm around his middle. "Why are you still awake?"

"I don't know. I dozed for a while." He kissed her forehead. Even after their workout she smelled so damn good.

"Go back to sleep. We'll have to get up in a couple of hours."

"Maybe."

He smiled. "Maybe?"

She yawned and nodded. "Maybe we'll stay in bed all day. I dare anyone to tell us we can't."

"Ah, Cass." He slid down so that she could rest her head on his chest. "What am I going to do with you?"

She lifted her head and looked at him. It was too dark to see her face, but she sounded too serious when she said, "Is that why you're awake? You're worrying about what to do with me?"

He didn't get what she meant at first, and then he sighed. "Don't start looking for hidden meanings or reading things into what I say." She stiffened against him, subtly retreating. He brought her close again and hugged her. "I am not worried about what to do with you."

"Good. You don't have to be."

He frowned. What did that mean? He almost

laughed out loud at himself. Talk about paranoid. "Let's both try to get some sleep, okay?"

She swirled her finger through his chest hair. "If you aren't tired yet…"

"Jesus, Cassie, you trying to put me in intensive care?"

She sighed and patted his chest. "I forgot. You are pushing thirty."

"Excuse me?"

She erupted into laughter.

He slid his hand between her thighs, immediately finding her heat, and the laughter died.

15

THE NEXT MORNING, while Dalton was in a male-bonding session, Cassie confirmed her appointment to see Bask after dinner. She didn't tell Dalton. She knew he'd give her a hard time. But seeing if she could get Bask to come on to her had been the original game plan, and since it was a good one, she was sticking to it.

Dalton thought their best avenue was through Simone. Cassie didn't discount either source. She thought they needed to exhaust all possibilities. And normally, she knew Dalton would agree.

She sighed as she folded her dirty clothes and stuffed them into a plastic laundry bag. Very mixed emotions plagued her over Dalton's sudden notion that she not try and lure Bask into temptation, so to speak. It was kind of nice that he felt so protective of her, even though he'd deny that was the reason, but that macho knucklehead attitude annoyed her, too. If he believed she was capable of handling her job, then she shouldn't be worried. Simple.

Sighing again, she sank to the edge of the bed, laid back and stared at the ceiling. Simple, hell. She'd blown it. She wasn't supposed to have fallen for him. Last night was supposed to have been a job perk. Not a night that replayed in her head so many times it made her dizzy.

So many more qualities than she'd ever imagined made up Dalton Styles. He was smart, funny, considerate, tender and when he was turned on…

She shivered, thinking about how skilled he was at touching a woman's body, finding just the right spot to drive her insane. How tempted she'd been to ask how many women he'd been with, but of course she hadn't dared. Not only did the timing stink, but she didn't want to fuel his worries.

Something was bothering him. She really didn't think it was regret. In fact, she was the one who had to kick him out of bed and order him into the shower. She smiled thinking of how he'd tried to drag her in with him. Which would never have worked. They'd already practically missed breakfast.

The amazing thing was, she felt so comfortable around him, as if she'd known him for a long time. Some people talked about old souls, and having crossed paths in other lives. She'd never believed any of that stuff. But the familiarity and comfort level they shared had her a little creeped out. In a good kind of way, but still…

Someone knocked at the door and she sprung to a sitting position. Tasha, probably, to tidy the room, but Cassie had already made the bed.

She opened the door, ready to tell Tasha to skip their room, but it was Simone. "Hi."

"Can I come in?" Simone sniffed, and then dabbed her nose with a tissue. Her eyes were red and puffy.

"Of course." Cassie stepped aside. "Take the chair. Can I get you some water?"

"No, thanks." She sat down. "I changed my mind. I would like some water. And would you happen to have an aspirin?"

"I'm sure I do." Cassie got her a glass of water first and then went into the bathroom to root through her cosmetic bag.

Simone had missed breakfast altogether and it was obvious why. She looked terrible. Either lack of sleep or a hangover had her looking older and more pathetic. Cassie couldn't help but feel a pang of sympathy for the older woman, but what an opportunity. As long as Bask didn't know where Simone was, Cassie had a great shot at getting some information.

"Here you go." She held out the bottle of tablets.

Simone shook out three into her palm and downed them with half a glass of water. "Thanks." She sniffed and then gave Cassie a shaky smile. "You're probably wondering what the hell I'm doing here."

"Uh…" Cassie shrugged and sat on the bed. "Yeah, actually I am."

Simone nibbled on her lower lip, looking hesitant suddenly as she studied the hem of her white cotton shirt. "I shouldn't have come."

"Something I said?" Lame remark, but Cassie hoped it would help relax her.

Simone glanced up, a frightened expression tugging at her brows. "Actually, yes."

"Huh?"

"Yesterday. During our open therapy session. I

liked what you said about marriage and partnership and all that.''

"Oh. I meant it.''

"I know. I could tell.'' Simone looked down again. "I admire that you know your mind. At your age, hell at my age, I've let myself be so easily swayed.''

"We all do that sometimes,'' Cassie said gently, her heart strings beginning to knot.

"Yes, but you're so strong. You tell Dalton what you want, what it takes for you to be happy. You don't accept crumbs just because he's your husband and that's the way things are. I think that's wonderful, Cassie. I think you're wonderful.''

God, she felt horrible. What a fraud! "Well, Dalton and I haven't been married long. It's easier to set the ground rules right off the bat. You and Grant, how long have you been married?''

Simone abruptly looked away and stood. "I need to go.''

Cassie stood, too. "I'm sorry. What did I say?''

"Nothing.'' Simone shook her head. "Nothing at all—I just need to go.''

"Oh. I thought you wanted to talk. You know, just kind of girl to girl.''

"I do. I did.'' Simone let out a sob and sank back down into the chair. "Grant isn't my husband,'' she whispered.

Cassie tried to look surprised. "But—but—''

"I'm married to someone else.''

That really did surprise Cassie. "Okay. Um, where is he?''

"I can't tell you that.'' Simone sighed and slouched

in the chair. "It's very complicated. Our marriage has become more of a business arrangement."

When the discovery registered, Cassie did all she could to stay contained. She took several deep calming breaths, even pinched herself on the leg to keep from saying or doing something incredibly stupid.

Simone was Bask's wife and they'd missed the whole damn thing. It made perfect sense. The two of them working together on the con. Who would he trust more than his own wife?

Cassie's adrenaline climbed as another realization struck her. If Bask and Simone were married, that made him a bigamist. He was legally married to Cassie's client, Marianne, and who knew how many other women.

True, bigamy didn't have the same legal ramifications as fraud, but the charge would at least keep him behind bars until they could persuade other women to come forward. Dalton said there was a client list and…

"I don't know why I'm telling you all this." Simone stared at her with misgiving. "I really don't. I guess I've bottled up so much for so long."

Cassie forced her attention back to the sniffling woman. She really did look awful, and Cassie suddenly hated the case. The idea that she was about to add more pain to the woman's life made her nauseous. But then she remembered that Simone was as guilty as Bask in swindling dozens of needy, vulnerable widows and divorcées.

"I'm happy to talk to you," Cassie said. "I know sometimes I just need to talk out loud to give myself some perspective. But don't you think your husband should be here for this marriage encounter—''

Simone half laughed, half sobbed.

Watching her closely, Cassie added, "Maybe you should talk to Mr. Blankenship about this."

Simone looked at her as if she were crazy. Pushing a hand through her tangled hair, she stood. "I have to go."

"To talk to Mr. Blankenship, I hope?"

The devastation on the other woman's face made Cassie regret fueling the fire. But then the old hardness was back and Simone's lips lifted in a cold smile. "Yeah, I'll think about it. I'm sure the great Mr. Blankenship will fix everything."

She headed for the door, and then stopped with her hand on the knob. "I wasn't here, okay?"

Cassie shrugged. "Sure."

"I mean it," Simone said, looking lost and frightened again. "No one can know I was here. Or about what I've told you. It's important."

"Got it."

Simone hesitated, regret evident in her expression, in the slump of her shoulders. "Thanks, Cassie," she murmured, and then left.

Damn. Amazing how two words could make Cassie feel like the lowest life form on earth. This part of the job was new to her and she knew she'd have to get through it without getting sappy. No matter how sorry she felt for Simone, the woman was still a criminal.

Cassie checked her watch, anxious for Dalton to return. According to today's schedule, the session would last another twenty minutes.

Her heart still raced and she went to her suitcase and dug around until she found the small notebook she'd brought. She needed to be able to remember everything Simone said. Jotting down a few notes wouldn't hurt. Not when her entire nervous system had gone haywire.

She checked her watch again. She couldn't wait to talk to Dalton.

SHE COULDN'T BELIEVE she'd dozed off, but she must have. The door closed softly and she slowly opened her eyes. Dalton smiled as he came toward her.

"Don't get up." He sat at the edge of the bed and laid a hand on her shoulder when she tried to lift herself up. "I'm thinking about crawling in and taking a nap myself."

She stifled a yawn and glanced at the digital clock. "Won't they expect us to come down for lunch?"

He lowered his head to nuzzle her neck. "If you're hungry, I'll take care of you."

She laughed. "I'm sure you would. Mmm..." She liked it when he licked that particular spot, right behind her ear, and then lightly bit her lobe. "How was your session?"

"A bunch of bullshit."

"Well, that describes it well." She moved over so he could lie down beside her. "Did you guys talk?"

"Hell, no."

"Silly me. A bunch of guys in a room with no football on the tube…. God forbid you should have anything to say to one another."

"Very sexist remark, honey. But that reminds me

that I did hear a new joke this morning. What did the blonde do when—''

She clamped a hand over his mouth. ''Don't you dare say it.''

''Why?'' His voice came out garbled but he didn't remove her hand. Instead he licked her palm.

She pulled it back. ''Dammit, that tickles.''

He grinned and laid his hand familiarly on her left breast, kneading gently, and making her thoughts scramble like crazy. ''It's a good joke. You'll laugh. I promise.''

''Unlike you, I had a very productive morning.'' She shifted to make him stop. She knew damn well where the touching would lead and she wanted to tell him about Simone first.

He gave her an odd look, a kind of wounded look that tugged at her heart. She kissed him, lightly, enough to reassure but not excite. ''Business before pleasure. Remember?''

''Sure.'' Briefly, he kissed her back. ''I thought by productive you meant you slept most of the morning.''

She gave him a smug smile. Wait till he heard... ''I had a chat with Simone.''

''Yeah? Without Bask butting in?''

''Yep, she came to our room.''

That got his interest. He shifted to his side to look at her, his brows drawn together.

''Simone is Bask's wife.''

He drew his head back, shock blanketing his face. ''She told you that?''

''No, but she told me enough that there isn't any doubt.'' She went on to repeat her conversation with

Simone, disappointed that he didn't seem more excited.

He didn't say anything for a long time after she'd finished, just stared toward the window.

"Well, what do you think?" she finally asked.

Exhaling a sigh, he ran a hand through his hair in several quick successions. "I should've seen that one."

"Not necessarily. Are all con artists who work together married?"

One side of his mouth lifted in a wry smile. "Well, at the very least, that makes our boy a bigamist. He is legally married to your client, correct?"

Cassie nodded. "Which means we can have him picked up and booked."

Dalton seemed doubtful, judging by the face he made. "We could if we thought he might bolt."

"If Simone looks as if she's losing it, he could get nervous and do just that."

"On the other hand, even if Simone does fall apart, he could simply remove her. There's no reason for him to be nervous or suspicious."

"True."

"Unless you think Simone might confess what she's told you."

"No, I really don't think she will." Cassie thought a minute. "Before she left she was adamant that I not tell anyone she'd even come to the room. Anyway, she didn't tell me anything specific. If we didn't know what we did about Bask, there's no way we would suspect he was her husband."

"You're right."

"Of course I am." She snuggled closer. "Get used to it."

He slowly turned her way and gave her an enigmatic look that had her thoughts forking off. Did he think she was implying there was a future for them? Or was he thinking she was just being smug? She hoped the latter was to his thinking. She could deal with being smug.

She sighed. She'd forgotten how complicated this relationship stuff could be. Not that she thought they were forging a relationship, she reminded herself, and sighed again.

He nudged her shoulders and when she lifted them, he slid his arm beneath her and pulled her close. "What's all that sighing for?"

"Just trying to figure out what we should do," she lied.

"Yeah, I know." He kissed her temple. "Well, I don't think we should make a move yet."

"Why?" She swallowed. Was he thinking the same thing she was? That the case would be over, and so would their association.

"As long as they aren't suspicious, I say we gather as much dirt as we can. Put that bastard away until he's too old to sweet-talk any more women out of their savings."

"I like it." Not because that gave her more time with Dalton. She really believed he was right. She did. "So we...wait?" She'd almost blown it. Or maybe he wouldn't be so against her meeting alone with Bask now. She decided not to test the water.

"We wait and hope Simone provides more information or is enough of a distraction to Bask that he slips up and does something stupid.''

''Speaking of distractions...'' Cassie smiled and slid her hand up Dalton's shirt. His nipples beaded under her restless fingers.

''What about lunch?'' He put a hand at her waist and toyed with the elastic of her shorts, dipping his fingers in to stroke her belly, withdrawing, and then dipping again, going lower each time.

She threw her leg across his thighs. He was already hard.

''Screw lunch,'' she said and reached for his buckle.

Chuckling, he pulled down her shorts, taking her panties with them.

She barely managed to pull off his belt and unsnap his jeans before he got up on his knees, freed the shorts from around her ankles and cast them aside. He tugged up the hem of her blouse and she lifted herself enough for him to pull it over her head.

She laid back waiting for him to unsnap the front of her bra. Instead, he spread her thighs and moved in between her knees.

''Dalton?'' She tensed, not understanding. Until he lowered his head and laved her with his tongue.

She grabbed two fistfuls of the quilt and held her breath. His tongue was hot and thorough, and she came so damn fast she didn't know what hit her.

HE SHADED his eyes and looked up at the stately white house. Lunchtime. Everyone would be in the dining room. He had the routine down by now.

No one would be more pleased than him when this

was over. He hated being outside in the hot sun most of the day. Good thing it wasn't the middle of summer. He would've begged off the assignment. Except he was perfect for the role, even he had to admit.

Damn stereotypes. Of course he'd end up with a major collar after this bust. Maybe even a promotion so he wasn't complaining…too much.

After making sure no one was around, he reached into his baggy pants' pocket and got out his cell phone. He hit speed dial, he sat on a lawn chair and uncapped a bottle of water while he waited. Before he could take a sip, his partner answered on the other end.

He took a quick sip anyway, and then said, "Tonight's the night. I'm sure." He paused to let his partner voice his concerns. The guy was a worrier. Out in the field he sucked, but he did a damn good job of tracking details and organizing raids.

"Bask has no history of violence and I don't expect any trouble. But if we hit in the middle of the night everyone will be asleep and that'll keep things simple. Line up the guys for midnight."

He gave Lenny a few more details and then hung up. Pushing off the chair, he mopped his sweaty forehead with a red bandana, and then grabbed the rake.

Yep, Sgt. Hamada was going to be damn glad when this bust was over.

16

CASSIE SAT ACROSS Bask's desk and waited for him to get off the phone. When he'd received a call five minutes into their private session she'd hoped she'd be able to overhear something useful.

No luck. He listened mostly, giving a few yes and no answers occasionally. He kept his gaze on her, a ghost of a smile on his lips. It creeped her out and she looked around his room to avoid his eyes.

The last time she'd been in here she hadn't noticed the sparseness of the office décor. A couple of pictures hung on the walls similar to the generic kind that you'd find in a hotel room. Even the furniture looked as if it might have been rented. It wasn't bad quality, but something he wouldn't mind leaving in a hurry.

On the wall behind his desk hung a license to counsel and a certificate of excellence awarded to him by a university she'd never heard of, and which probably didn't exist.

When she finally brought her gaze back to him, he was still watching her intently. He smiled, and then put up a finger, indicating he'd be only a moment longer.

She smiled back, trying to figure out what she might

have thought of him if she didn't know what a scumbag he was. Most women found him good-looking, obviously, and she probably would have as well, even though she didn't particularly find fair men attractive.

His light blue eyes were almost hypnotic and his smile disarming. He had that special way of making a woman feel as if she were the only one in the room once he made eye contact with her. Cassie had seen Zelda melt into a puddle with him more than once, and it was really sad and annoying how she constantly seemed to seek his approval. Kathy wasn't too bad around him. Yet.

"I apologize for the interruption, Cassie," Bask said, smiling, as he replaced the receiver. "Cassie—is that short for Cassandra?"

She nodded.

"A family name?"

"My grandmother's."

"Cassandra is a beautiful name. Do you mind if I call you that?"

It was almost painful to smile but she managed. "I'd like that."

"You're probably wondering why I asked to see you privately."

That was news to her. She'd made the appointment with Mary Jane. "Actually, I asked to see you, as well."

He lifted a brow. "Oh?"

She wished she'd kept her mouth shut and let him talk. "Why did you want to see me?"

"I wasn't happy with the way we left our last conversation. I didn't want you to think I was ignoring you."

"Not at all. I listened to your advice. Went back to massage class, and I still think my husband's the biggest buffoon this side of Dallas." She sighed, and added, "I can't see trying anymore. I do have some of my own money from a trust fund. Plus the pre-nup I signed will take care of me quite well."

Bask gave her a condescending smile. "Actually, I think you're wrong."

"What?"

"You two not only have a great deal of chemistry but I sense you have a lot of trust in each other. And respect. Both very important in a relationship."

"You've got to be kidding."

"Be honest with yourself, Cassandra. You may not always like Dalton's behavior or share his chauvinistic ideas, but you know he's a good man and you can count on him."

Cassie didn't respond. This was not good. Not good at all. What was she supposed to go back and tell Dalton? That they were perfect for each other? This was not good.

"You look upset," Bask said, getting up from his chair and coming around the desk.

She braced herself. Maybe this was it—the big consolation move. He'd put his arms around her and tell her not to fret and how he'd...

He perched at a respectable distance on the edge of his desk and took her hands instead. "Cassandra, look me in the eyes and tell me you wouldn't care what happened to Dalton.''

"Of course I care. That isn't the point. I just don't want to live with him.'' She tried to look convincing.

"All right, my fault, I phrased that wrong. How would you feel if you never saw him again after this week?''

She couldn't breathe for a moment and she squeezed his hands. Tight. Too tight. She let go while forcing herself to breathe. "I'm sure I'd still see him…''

"Because you couldn't bear not to.''

"No.'' She didn't have to pretend this time.

"Cassandra?''

She wanted to push him away. Get up and run out of his office. She probably *wouldn't* see Dalton again. Maybe in court, if it came to that, but that would be the extent of any future association. He'd be off on another assignment in a matter of days.

The thought made her sick to her stomach.

Robert nudged her chin up. "Why are you resisting?'' he asked, watching her closely. "You still want him.''

"I don't.'' Damn, she was blowing it. "I mean, I do. Physically. We do great in that department.'' She exhaled slowly. "But that isn't enough. I want more.''

"What is it you want, Cassandra?'' He took her hands again and leaned closer.

His breath hit her cheek and she flinched. He backed off. The move was subtle, but she knew she'd blown it. If she wanted him to hit on her, she'd have to make the next overture.

Dammit.

"I'm sorry if I seem skittish," she said quickly. "I didn't tell him I was meeting with you and he can have quite a temper."

"Don't worry. He knows not to rock the boat while you two are here. This is his chance to save the marriage." He smiled reassuringly. "I doubt he'll cause any trouble."

She tried to look impressed. "I really wish he were more like you...rational, calm, even-tempered."

"That's my job." He held her gaze for a long unnerving moment. "What is it you want from me, Cassandra?"

"From you?"

He nodded, his eyes probing and hypnotic. "How can I help you?"

"Well, I don't know." She stared back, rational thought deserting her. She didn't want to sound too suggestive or pushy, just needy. "I was hoping for some guidance or advice." Sniffing, she looked away and dabbed at her eyes. They were as dry as a bone but he didn't know that. "Frankly, Robert, I don't know what to do."

He reached for her hand again, and surprised her by urging her to her feet. She stood but he didn't move back to give her room. He took her face in his hands and asked, "Do you trust me?"

"I suppose," she said, not wanting to sound too eager. Her heart pounded so hard it echoed in her ears. "Yes, I do."

"Good." He smiled and moved his head a fraction.

Hell, was he going to kiss her?

A sudden knock at the door stopped him cold.

He slackened his hold and drew back slightly, annoyance darkening his eyes. "Who is it?"

"Robert? It's Zelda."

Panic flashed in his face. He quickly lowered his hands, but before he could retreat, the door opened.

"I'm sorry to bother you, Robert, but—" Zelda stopped when she saw Cassie. She blinked, and then looked at Bask, her eyes filled with confusion and betrayal.

"Zelda." He hurried across the room and took her arm. "Come in, please."

"I didn't mean to interrupt you," she murmured, resisting his attempt to draw her inside.

"You haven't. Cassie needed some advice and now that I've given her something to ponder, we're actually finished." He looked at Cassie for confirmation.

She shrugged, trying to think fast. Trying not to be swayed by the devastation on Zelda's face. "Yes, you've been helpful. I think Dalton and I—" She broke off and stepped away from the desk. "Anyway, I'll think about what you said and we can talk later."

Still looking uncomfortable, Zelda let Bask lead her toward the couch.

"Well, isn't this cozy?"

Simone's voice, slurred and caustic, drew everyone's attention. She stood at the door, a drink in her hand, her hair and makeup-smeared face a mess.

Cassie's gaze shot to Bask. His face was a mask of panic and anger.

"Later, Simone," he said sternly. "We'll talk later."

"Sure, honey." She drained the amber contents in her glass. "We always have to talk later. I'm always last in line." She advanced into the room. "Guess what, lover, I'm tired of it."

"Simone." Bask started toward her, but then glanced at Cassie. "We'll talk again tomorrow afternoon," he said in a tone that implied he wanted her to leave.

Cassie tried to smile. This was *perfect.* Simone looked angry and upset enough to spill her guts. And with Zelda as a witness. Perfect. An idea struck her suddenly.

"Let go of my arm, Robert." Simone jerked away from him.

"I can come back tomorrow, as well," Zelda said, and scurried around Cassie.

"That's an excellent idea," Bask said, his furious gaze fastened to Simone. "Good night, ladies."

"Wait," Cassie said loudly. Everyone looked at her. She wished she knew what to say. "You aren't leaving for Rio tomorrow, are you? Or is that next week?"

"Rio?" Simone snapped her gaze back to him. "You son of a bitch."

"I don't know what she's talking about," Robert said calmly, but he couldn't conceal the panic in his eyes, the desperate way he tried to tug Simone farther into the room.

"Please, ladies, you need to leave."

"Robert?" Zelda looked confused and frightened.

"When are you going to Rio? You said we'd..." Her voice trailed off as her gaze travelled to Simone and then Cassie.

"Obviously this is a misunderstanding. I'm not going to Rio tomorrow or any other day." His murderous glare dared Cassie to contradict him. But there was fear in his eyes as well, a desperation that made Cassie uneasy. "I have no idea where you got that information, Cassandra."

"It all makes sense now." Simone shook her head, looking dazed. "You're leaving me and going to Rio. You ungrateful bastard." She tried to take a swing at him, but Bask caught her arm.

He jerked her hard. "Simone, you're making a big mistake."

"My mistake was marrying you, you greedy bastard. Ouch! Let go of me."

Zelda gasped. "Robert, what is she talking about?"

Cassie stepped in to help free Simone from his clearly painful grip of her arm. "I suggest you let her go before I call Dalton to convince you."

Something sparked in Bask's eyes, something far more alarming than fear or panic as his gaze bore into Cassie. "Who are you?"

"Let the lady go."

Dalton stood in the doorway, his voice low and threatening, his expression almost predatory.

Bask pushed Simone away and made a dash for his desk.

Oh, God. For a gun? Cassie lunged after him. She

vaguely heard Dalton yell for her to get out of the way, and then a loud crash startled everyone.

Seconds later three men with guns burst through the door. One of them was the gardener. A badge hung from around his neck. He held it up to Bask. "Robert Bask, you're under arrest for embezzlement and fraud."

"UNBELIEVABLE." Dalton used a pithy four-letter word he'd never used in front of her before. He threw his shirts, unfolded, into his suitcase. "I blew it. I friggin' blew it. Higgins is going to love this."

Cassie quietly folded her own clothes and laid them on the bed between their suitcases. She hadn't said much. Anger radiated from him like heat from a volcano. None of it directed at her, but she hated seeing him beat himself up like he had for the past twenty minutes.

"Shit, I bet Higgins already knows." He stopped throwing in clothes and stared blankly at the open suitcase, his expression growing angrier. "The son of a bitch had to know Bunko was working on the case."

"Then why would he assign you?"

"I'd just wrapped up a case. I was free and had the resources...."

"Do you cross departmental lines like this often?"

"We try not to. Anyway, this was about penance."

She had no idea what he was talking about, and wasn't sure she wanted to ask right now as she watched him clench his jaw, shake his head in self-disgust.

"Dalton." She laid a hand on his arm.

He shook her off. "Don't patronize me, okay?"

She drew back. "Since when am I the enemy?"

"You're not." He exhaled sharply and scrubbed at his face. "I'm sorry. This has nothing to do with you."

Cassie retreated, both physically and emotionally. His remark shouldn't have stung, but it did. He didn't owe her any explanation just because they'd made love. She knew the score. Sex had been a perk while they investigated Bask. But now that was over.

She turned back to her suitcase and started packing the clothes she'd folded, trying to shake the melancholy crawling over her.

"Hey, I really am sorry." Dalton tried to get her attention but she wouldn't look up. She didn't trust herself to meet his gaze. "You're the one who figured out about Simone," he said. "Got information out of Zelda. Shit, if Hamada hadn't come in when he had, Simone would have been singing like a canary and Bask would be wearing *my* handcuffs right now."

A surge of pleasure loosened her tension and she slanted him a look. He sure didn't seem any less tense. The self-recrimination in his eyes chilled her.

"I'm the one who screwed up," he said, grabbing a pair of jeans and slamming them into his suitcase. "A nothing case like this and I screw up. Unbelievable."

She stiffened. "I wouldn't call it a nothing case."

"Right. A friggin' first-year academy cadet could have wrapped this fluff case up in two days."

Hurt and angry, she looked away, struggling for re-straint.

Nothing case? No wonder she'd done such a good job. Screw him.

"Cassie?"

"What?" She threw the rest of her neatly folded clothes in a sloppy pile and closed her suitcase. The police had told everyone to vacate the house within fifteen minutes and that was fine with her.

"It's too late to drive back to Midland." He reached for her suitcase but she grabbed it first. His gaze narrowed. "There's a motel about five miles from—"

"I'd rather go back tonight," she interrupted. "I'll drive if you're too tired."

"Honey, what's wrong?"

Cassie took a calming breath, stopped and turned around when she got to the door. "You accuse me of being patronizing?

"You tell me what a great job I did—did you mean for a rookie? Or maybe I didn't do too badly for a dumb blonde?"

"Hey, come on, Cassie." What he'd said registered in his face. And then regret. Too late. "You know better."

"I thought I did." She left and started down the stairs.

She heard voices coming from the first floor and wished like hell she could take another way out of the house.

Zelda and Harvey and Tom and Kathy all waited with their suitcases in the parlor. A pale and stricken

Mary Jane sat in the corner bring questioned by one of the officers. Cassie had already learned from Hamada that they didn't suspect Mary Jane was in on the con. She was just another pawn who'd fallen for Bask's charm.

Cassie made way for two agents carrying out Bask's computer. Right behind them was Dalton. She hurried toward the front door, trying to avoid him, which was stupid since they still had to ride back in the same car.

She got outside and saw Bask sitting in the back seat of an unmarked white sedan. Simone stood outside the car next to Hamada, her hands cuffed behind her back. As soon as she saw Cassie she started to laugh.

"You know why Zelda was the pigeon and not you?" she called out to Cassie. "You're gonna love this." Simone laughed again. "Robert thought he didn't have a chance with you. He said you and Dalton were too tight. Too much in love. Nothing would break you two up." Still laughing, she used her shoulder to wipe her nose. "And you turn out to be cops."

Cassie said nothing. Out of the corner of her eye, she saw that Dalton had come up behind her. He'd obviously heard. That ought to lift his mood, make him laugh.

God, she did not want to drive back with him.

"We'll be locking up the house now," Hamada said as everyone filed out in sheepish silence. "Got everything out?" The looks on Tom, Kathy and Zelda's faces tore at Cassie. They'd arrived trusting Bask, hoping he'd help repair their marriages. At least Cassie had known what she was getting into.

She bit her lower lip. No, she hadn't. She hadn't expected to fall in love. And damn, she hadn't expected Dalton to be like all the rest. Screw him. She was a good investigator. And if this was such a fluff case, why were their four agents involved? No matter, his words still stung. She gripped her suitcase tighter and lifted her chin.

"Thanks for everyone's cooperation," Hamada said. "We'll be in touch. Everyone okay? You all have rides?"

Before Cassie even knew what she'd done, she waved at him. "Sergeant, if it's not too much trouble, I could use one." She didn't dare so much as glance back at Dalton.

"THAT'S THE TROUBLE with you, Styles. You think rules and regulations are made for other people." Hector leaned back in his black leather chair and locked his hands behind his head, his smug, superior expression burning a hole in Dalton's gut. "I hope the Bask fuck-up taught you a lesson."

Dalton sat in the designated seat across from his boss, and then swung his feet up onto Higgins's desk, mostly because he knew it pissed him off.

"But you didn't expect me to collar Bask."

Hector's gaze narrowed. "What do you mean?"

"You just wanted me out of the way for a week."

"I don't know who you've been talking to but—"

"Come on, Hector, I know you. We go way back.

You wanted me out of the way while you lobbied for a nomination.''

"That's absurd." Hector unnecessarily pushed his glasses up the bridge of his nose, a nervous habit he'd had for as long as Dalton could remember.

"What did you do, imply I was on suspension?"

"Where are you coming up with all this nonsense?"

Dalton knew he was right. He could see it written all over Hector's face. "See, I know I present a problem for you. On the one hand, my successful arrest record has made you look damn good. But my unconventional methods, which account for my success I might point out, have called too much attention to the bureau. And you."

"You screwed up, Styles." Hector's face turned red. "Admit it and quit dancing around the issue by fabricating a bunch of bullshit."

"I admit I screwed up." His thoughts went to Cassie. He'd only talked to her once since Bask's arrest a week ago. About the case. The conversation had been brief. She hadn't been angry or sarcastic. Just sad. It tore at his heart. "I botched a simple case…a case I should never have been assigned. What happened, Hector? Getting the bad guys used to be just as important to you. More important than private agendas."

He put up a silencing finger. "If you shut up right now, I won't have the Bask incident documented in your file."

Dalton stared at his old friend. All Dalton ever wanted to be was a good agent, and at one time a good husband and father. He'd failed at the husband part.

And lately he hadn't been a particularly good agent. So who the hell was he anymore?

"Tell you what, Hector," he said, swinging his boots off the desk. "You do whatever you want. I quit."

"You can't do that." Hector's fists clenched as he glared in warning.

"You'll receive my formal resignation tomorrow." Dalton smiled as he stood. "All typed up nice and neat just like it should be."

17

CASSIE STRETCHED out on her back on the couch and placed the bowl of popcorn on her stomach. This was her second serving with extra butter and she knew she'd end up feeling sick. But her bigger concern was what the hell she'd done with the remote control.

Over the past week she'd gotten hooked on *Days of Our Lives* and she couldn't stand it if she didn't find out what happened between Roman and Marlena. Or maybe her name was Kristen...

Pathetic. Cassie had made it through college without once getting involved in a soap opera like all her friends had, and now she planned her days around them. They'd become a distraction she craved like chocolate on certain days.

It was all Dalton's fault. She wished she'd never met the jerk.

She put the popcorn aside and searched between the sofa cushions for the remote. Tomorrow Jennifer had another case for her to start. She would accept it of course, even though she didn't have much heart for tailing a suspected cat burglar, who also happened to be the son of a prominent politician.

It was a touchy case that needed to remain low profile until Cassie could provide substantial evidence. That Jen had that much faith in Cassie should have made her feel good. But Dalton's dissertation on what a nothing case the Bask investigation had been still rang in Cassie's ears.

Dalton had called once, tried to make amends in a roundabout way by asking unnecessary questions about the case, but the sting hadn't ebbed. The fact that he'd made no attempt to see her proved that he wasn't all that concerned about her feelings. It also meant it was over. They were over. Of course they'd never promised each other anything more than a week's fling.

She sniffed. So why did the thought of not seeing him again hurt so damn much? She missed his sexy smile, and the way he could make her laugh. And God, but she missed his touch....

Nope. She couldn't go there. That was trouble. Big trouble.

She dabbed at her misty eyes and spotted the remote wedged between the *TV Guide* and the pink throw pillow her mother had made eons ago. Cassie aimed the remote at the television, turned on the tube and then got back into position with the bowl of popcorn.

She'd barely gotten comfortable again when the doorbell rang. Startled, she jerked upright and popcorn flew everywhere.

"Dammit!" She didn't care about the mess, but now she'd have to make another batch. And melt more butter.

Cassie unlocked the deadbolt and mentally chastised

herself for forgetting to use the peephole as she started to open the door. If it was a salesman, he'd be sorry he stopped at her door. Although it was probably the courier Jen used to...

"Dalton?" Her hand flew to her hair. One big tangled mop. "What are you doing here?"

"I guess I should have called, huh?" He gave her an unapologetic smile. "Can I come in?"

She thought about the blanket of popcorn all over her couch and floor. "Oh, brother."

His smile vanished. He shoved his hands into the pockets of his jeans and moved back a little. She'd never seen him look so uncertain. Butterflies fluttered in her chest.

"Come in," she said, sighing, and hoping he didn't see her hand tremble as she swung the door open wider. "At your own risk."

He frowned but stepped inside. When he saw the popcorn sprayed across the carpet he choked back a laugh. "What happened?"

"The doorbell startled me."

He peered at a clump before he removed it to sit down. "Too bad. Lots of butter. Just how I like it."

"The kitchen is right there." She gestured, amazed that she could appear so calm when her heart raced a mile a minute. "Help yourself."

Dalton had already focused on the television. *Days of Our Lives* had just started. "I thought I was going to miss this episode. Roman hasn't admitted to where he's been the last month yet, has he?"

Cassie stared at him. "You watch soap operas?"

He gave her a sheepish shrug. "Just this past week."

"I thought you'd be on another assignment by now."

"I quit."

She continued to stare at him, even though he seemed suddenly absorbed with the TV. "You quit?"

He nodded. "You have a Coke or beer or anything?"

Ignoring the popcorn, she sank down next to him. "Why?"

"Kind of a long story."

"I have time."

He rubbed his jaw, the back of his neck. "I needed a change."

"That's not a long story."

He turned to look at her. "I'm sorry, Cassie. You did a really good job with the Bask case. I screwed up, and I tried to downplay it by downplaying the case. I was wrong. My ego got in the way."

She'd pretty much guessed that in her more rational moments, but it was good to hear it come from him. "You didn't quit over that."

"No, but the whole thing helped me see some truths about myself. All I ever wanted to do was be a good cop. And good husband. I failed at that part, and I couldn't let myself fail at my job. At any cost. Until it cost me you."

Her stomach flipped over. She took his hand.

He smiled. "Cassie, I know we haven't known each

other long. And we didn't get off to the best start, but I feel this connection with you I can't explain."

She nodded. "Me, too."

"Yeah?" His smile broadened.

"Yeah. So what now?"

"I'm moving to Midland."

Her breathing stopped altogether.

"I have money saved until I get a job and then—"

She threw her arms around his neck and kissed him so hard he fell backward. Popcorn crunched beneath him making them both smile. And then he deepened the kiss, using his tongue to part her lips, and then slowly sweeping the inside of her mouth.

When they finally came up for air, he said, "I'm going to take that as approval."

She laughed. "That would be a safe bet."

"I love you, Cassie."

She swallowed. "I love you, too."

He got a serious look on his face and held her gaze steady. "I have one for you."

"What?"

"What did the blonde say—"

She gasped and put her hands over her ears. "I can't believe you're saying this. You—"

He pried her hands away. "What did the blonde say when the cop asked her to marry him?"

"You pain in the—" She blinked. "Dalton..."

"The blonde probably wanted to think about it, probably go slow and take some time...."

"The hell she did." Cassie kissed him again, and this time they weren't so quick to come up for air.

Epilogue

"I HAVE A PROPOSITION for you." Jennifer sat at her desk with her swollen feet up, her gaze on Dalton as he fed Annie her bottle.

Cassie watched him, too. She loved seeing him with the baby. He was such a natural it gave her a warm fuzzy feeling.

"Dalton, I want you to join the agency." Jennifer rubbed her very pregnant belly. "I can't pay you what you made with the government but if the cases keep pouring in the way they have, that could change." Jen smile slyly. "Plus, we don't have many rules around here."

Dalton stared at her. Annie noisily sucked the nipple trying to get more juice.

Cassie had known the offer was coming. Jen had asked her first if Dalton working with her would be a problem. Yeah, right, as if... "Here," Cassie said, when he still looked a little dumbfounded. "Give me Annie."

He passed her the baby. "You really have enough cases?"

"Are you kidding? We're swamped. You know how hard I've been working Cassie this past month."

Dalton smiled and then turned to Cassie. "Honey, what do you think?"

"I think if we ever want to see each other you'd better say yes."

"Good." Jen was back to business, looking at her calendar. "Let's see…your wedding is in two weeks. Heck, no reason you couldn't start tomorrow, right?" She pulled out a hefty stack of file folders. "Take your pick."

Cassie stared in disbelief. "Those are all pending cases?"

"I started getting behind again when Zach left." A wry smile curved Jen's lips. "At least I know you guys won't be leaving me to get married."

Dalton picked up the first two folders and leafed through them. "Hmm…" He scanned the notes. "We can get this one knocked out in a couple of days."

Cassie and Jen exchanged amused glances. He certainly wasn't lacking in confidence.

"Here, Cass." He handed her the folder. "You take this one. Possible insurance fraud."

She blinked. "The one we could knock out in a couple of days?"

"Yeah, you could handle this with one hand tied behind your back."

She felt that flutter of pride his faith in her prompted.

"You'll be working on another case?"

He nodded, already busy studying the contents of the next file.

She glanced at Jen who beamed from ear to ear.

''You guys have just made my day,'' she said and then grimaced. Her hand went to her stomach. ''Oh-oh.''

Dalton looked up.

''What?'' Cassie moved closer.

''I'm not sure but—'' Jen winced again. ''Okay, now I'm sure. Who wants to drive me to the hospital?''

''Oh, shit!''

Both women looked at Dalton. He set down the folder, his face as white as a sheet.

Jen laughed. ''Looks like you're driving, Cass.''

''This is early. You have a bag ready?''

''In the closet.''

Cassie looked at Dalton. ''Can you hold Annie?''

He nodded and reached for the baby without a word. Probably, Cassie suspected, because he couldn't speak. She hid a smile as she went for the bag. Her big, hunky, macho husband-to-be looked scared out of his wits.

Was it possible that she could suddenly love him twice as much?

Holding Annie in one arm, he used his other to help Jen to her feet. ''Don't worry about a thing, boss,'' he said, and kissed her cheek.

If you enjoyed what you just read,
then we've got an offer you can't resist!

Take 2 bestselling
love stories FREE!
Plus get a FREE surprise gift!

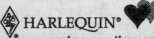